My Hood
My Way

My Hood My Way
Copyright © 2015 by Kenee Triplett

ISBN (_____)

Printed in USA by

Dedication

I like to Dedicate dis book to my two brothers who' not here to see the man and writer dat i've became.. I know they wud be really proud of me so i like them to continue to watch over me as i strive to success, and i also want to thank my mother and father for making it possible for me to be breathing..i also want to thank all my supporters for the will to keep pushing me to

move forward with my dream.. I also wants to thank my woman sheena smith for holding me down even when it was times i didn't want to be helded and never giving up on me...also i want to thank Kadience Caniah Triplett my daughter for being my heart to will me off the streets before it was to late...i also want to thank my family for the love and comfort they always given me...i also want to thank the father himself cas it was his will to give me a soul to experience life....

4

Part One

"Wait till I get my money right oh, oh, oh, oh…" Bj was singing along with the Kanye West song that was playing on the radio as he drove up 55th and Garfield, heading to the gas station to get some cigars to go with the ounce of green he had just gotten from one of his homies named C. (but we call him Ace Boogie). As he was caught at the red light on 55th and Ashland waiting for it to turn green, he happens to look to the right in the direction of the liquor store and see some young cat making a few transactions with some crack heads. He gets furious instantly, at the sight of what's going on 'cause he done caught the lil dude twice this week serving and told him not to be serving in front of the liquor store 'cause it's not a free enterprise.

Bj Was so focused on the problem at hand that he didn't notice that the light had turned green ten seconds ago, until the people in the car behind him started to blow their horn. As he looked in the rearview mirror to see who was blowing their horn like they don't recognize his car, which is the only 4 door Chevy brougham sitting on 26 inch choppers with a custom paint job that changes to six different colors. It also has 9 inch TV's in all four headrest. He paid $6,000 to have all 4 doors converted to suicide doors (so they can come up instead of out).

He sees 2 cats in the car with their hats cocked hard to the

5

right, which lets him know that these 2 individuals are from a different gang. As he focuses hard on the driver, he senses trouble as he recognizes him as one of his enemies who he's been beefing with for the last 3 months over some drug turf that he took from them.

He reaches over to the ash tray and pushes the lighter in and turns the air conditioner all the way up. This activates his stash spot. This is the special spot he had installed when he did the other custom work. Instantly his stash spot jumps open. Bj reaches in it and grabs the chrome 40 cal Ruger that he "never leaves home without", especially for situations like this when he's in the car by himself and trouble is at his throat. He sits the chrome piece on his lap and sticks up his middle finger to try to get them to follow him into the gas station, where he would have the advantage because this is his turf also.

The cats then pull up closer as if they're going to ram him from behind but he pulls off and turns into the gas station. "Just as I had planned," he said to himself. He smiles as he watches his soon to be worm food in the rearview mirror.

He pulls up by the second pump and before he can put his car in park and take his foot off the brake the two cats are already out of their car and approaching his ride. As they get to the bumper of his car, Bj hops out of the car as if it were on fire.

The dudes, so bold and blind that they don't even see the gun in his hand that he is holding to his side out of easy view, Bj then snaps in a vicious tone of voice, "Who the f*ck y'all think y'all is. blowing y'all mother f*cking horn at me, in my hood at that, like y'all is crazy."

6

The driver of the car, who is about 6'6" and 190 lbs. responds "Bitch ass n*gga, who you think you're talking," and before he can finish his sentence, in one swift motion, Bj lifts his gun and fires one shot which enters the dude's mouth and exits out the back of his head. Before he even falls to the pavement, his friend takes off running but only makes it two steps before even reaching his car, he was granted a new breathing hole in the back of his head.

Bj then squats down and picks up the two shell casings in one swift motion and hops back in his ride. As he's leaving the gas station, he nods in the direction of the cashier and she nods back, which indicates that he will be back to pick up the surveillance tape of the drama that had just took place.

9 months later

It's in the middle of May, 2015 and the sun is beaming through the drapes that covers his sliding door to the balcony. He gets up out of bed slowly, not to wake his soon to be wife, Sheena, who is still sleeping with a light snore. He walks over to the door and takes a step onto the balcony to check the weather.

It feels like it's in the high 70's, as he sits there looking around for a few minutes at the back of his three bedroom condo in Hyde Park enjoying the view and happy of how much he has accomplished in less than a year.

It's the weekend and every weekend is for his family. He's taking Sheena and his daughter Tania to a early morning movie, to Hollywood Park and out to dinner. As he steps back in and heads toward the shower, he stops by Tania's room and peeks in.

She's still sleeping, like the angel she is, so he pulls the door back closed softly, so he wouldn't wake her.

After he finishes taking his shower, which felt so good that he stayed in there an hour longer than he usually does, he wraps the dry towel around him and exits the bathroom to the smell of one of his favorite meals of the day, breakfast. He mumbles to himself, while walking the hall towards his master bedroom, "That's why I'm in love with this woman."

As he enters this bedroom to dry himself off and put his clothes on, his cell phone starts ringing. He picks it up off the dresser and looks at the caller ID. He then mumbles to himself, "What the f*ck this b*tch wants this early in the morning?" He answers with aggression in his voice.

"What the f*ck is up meaka? You know not to be calling me early in the morning. That's why I treat you like I do now, 'cause you don't know how to listen. All you do is have your hands out and your ass tutted up to who ever going to give your trifling ass some money." He goes hard on her and hangs up the phone before she can get a word out.

Before he can put it back on the dresser, it starts ringing again. He answers it without looking at the caller ID. This time with a tone that can kill, "B*tch, what you think I'm joking with you…" The caller on the other end yells "Hold, Hold, Hold on bro." As Bj took a second to hear what was being said on the other end of the phone, he realizse it was his right hand man, "My fault, bro."

"This B*tch, meaka, been calling my horn this morning,"
"Yeah, bro"

"Hell, yeah, I done told her before not to be doing that, but f*ck her, What's up, bro?"

"Sh*t everything good this morning."

I just came from through the hood and I came across a lil problem but it's cool.

"What type of problem you're talking about?"

"B.J, I'm not going to talk on this phone, so I'll holler at you when you come outside."

"Nah, law, meet me at Wayne's Cajun in the mall on 55th and Dan Ryan in an hour. You know that sh*t will be on my mind all day until we talk."

"Alight, BJ." and then the phone went dead.

He thinks to himself as he gets dressed of what could be wrong. Sheena enters the room and sees him in a blank stare and notice something's wrong. "Good morning, is everything alright?"

"Yeah, I just got to go meet with White Boy this morning to discuss this morning's affairs. You and Nia gone get dressed. I'll be back to get y'all."

"Alright, but can you eat some food before you leave?" Sheena asks.

"Sure, make me a plate. I'll eat it while I'm driving."

After he finished getting dressed he headed down the stairs. He gave his daughter a kiss and a few tickles until she begged him to stop through laughing tears.

"Daddy will be back to get you and mommy" he grabs the plate off the kitchen table and headed for the door. He reaches on the stand and grabs Sheena's car keys to her 2007 Malibu that he bought her for her 24th birthday 2 months ago and exits the condo.

40 minutes later, he arrives at his destination. He sits in the car puffing on a blunt while he waits on his man to arrive. 10 minutes later his man pulls on the side of him. He's so busy daydreaming, which is something he does a lot when he's thinking hard, that he doesn't see him pull in the parking space next to him.

White Boy hops out and pulls on the door handle on the passenger side as if it's already open. Bj jumps and reached for his stash spot, until he looks up and sees who it is. He takes a deep breath as he realize he was caught slippin and hit the unlock button.

White Boy hops in and tells Bj, "You better stop slippin' like that before one day you meet your Maker, bro."

"Yeah, I know. I'm going to go see a doctor or something soon to see if I can get some medication for my daydreaming."

"An law, what the hell was you reaching for, like you got a stash in here?"

"I know right, but what's good?"

White Boy wastes no time getting to the point. "I was riding through the land this morning, you know. Just checking things out to make sure everything's running good, until I notice a lot of traffic going through the alley between Marshfield and Paulina. I ride through the alley and see a lot of our customers going through Junebug's yard and up to his back door.

"Junebug, who the hell is that?" BJ asked.

"You know crack head ass Junebug who be stealing cars.

10

"Oh you, talking about Auto June,"

"Yeah, that feind ass n*gga, but anyway, I sneak up to the back door as he was about to close it and kicks it open. He tried to run thinking I was the police or somebody."

I ran behind him and hit him in the back of the head with the butt of my .45 automatic. He starts screaming like a bitch, as he hits the floor holding his head. "Please don't kill me. You can have everything." was the words Junebug spoke. I pointed my gun at his head and demanded for him to look at me, as he turned around to see who I was, you could see death in his eyes."

"What the f*ck do you think you're doing selling $5 rocks out your crib? White Boy asks.

Junebug starts stuttering cause he is so scared. "I, I, wa, was told tha, that it, it was coo, cool, ma, man, please don't kill, kill mmm, me wh, whi, White Boy."

"Shut your b*tch ass up with all that whining and tell me who sh*t you're selling."

"Roger, who tall as Roger?"

"Yea, Yeah," Junebug said as he's still stuttering his ass off.

"You mean to tell me you let Roger's p*ssy ass trick you into serving out your crib?"

""Ok, this is what we're going to do. Call his b*tch ass and tell him that you're finished and you need some more quick. " White Boy tells Junebug, who does as he was told with no problem cause he knows if he don't, what would happen.

White Boy sits in the living room on the couch talking on his cell phone and watching Junebug shake uncontrollably as they wait for Roger to arrive. He then hears music playing loud out front. He closed his cell phone and peeks through the curtain and sees Roger getting out of his car.

He motions for Junebug to get the door while he stands off to the side with his gun cocked and aimed. Roger enters the apartment with a package in his hand. He sees a scary look on Junebug's face as the door shuts behind him, but it was too late as he was knocked unconscious from the blow to the back of his head. Another knock comes from the door.

White Boy opens the door, he already knows who it is because he was just talking to Scrap, who is the leader of one of his clean up crews. before Roger pulled up.

He gives them daps as they enter and gets right to business. "Tie these mother f*ckers up." was the words that White Boy barked at his crew. After tying them up, White Boy sits in front of Roger and Junebug smoking a blunt. The crew sits there patiently waiting for their boss to give the next order.

As he takes his last pull off the blunt, he gets up and walks over towards Roger and Junebug and blows the smoke in their faces. "I know y'all had to be high off something, but not that damn high to think that y'all can just open up shop and start grinding like y'all run sh*t around here. Huh?"

Roger tried to say something but the tape on his mouth stopped anything from coming out. "Smack" was all you heard from the hard slap when White Boy hit him.

"Shut your b*tch ass up p*ssy ass n*gga. I'm talking right now. If you wanted to talk you should have came and talked to us about opening up shop, but instead you was doing you and whatever you wanted to do, so now, I'm doing me!"

Scrap, who is the leader of the clean up crew, is high yellow, about 6' tall and 180 pounds of muscle, has a heart as vicious as a silver back gorilla. He was told to look around the house and find whatever he can find so White Boy can torture Roger and Junebug.

Junebug started squirming to get free as now he figures out that he's not going to make it out of this alive. Scrap returns with all type of tools in his hands.

White Boy grabs the meat cleaver and walks over to Roger. He beats his left hand three times and then his right hand three time as well. Blood starts dripping from the open cut on the top of his hand. White Boy then tells Taterbean, who is the oldest to Scrap, to go into the kitchen and get some salt.

While waiting on Taterbean to come back, he grabs the pliers off the floor and walks over to Junebug. His eyes get big as he knows its time for him to start feeling pain. He latches onto Junebug's thumbnail and pulls on it until the whole nail comes off. White Boy reaches for the salt from Taterbean. Roger and Junebug start squirming to get free as White Boy walks towards them with the salt in his hand. As he sprinkles salt on the open wounds of Roger's hands, Junebug starts shaking as if he is having a seizure. White Boy then pours some on Junebug's thumb and he passes out instantly from the burning.

After hours of ripping off earlobes, nipples, toe nails and breaking their arms and legs, Roger and Junebug sit in the chair motionless and eager to just be dead instead of suffering. White Boy finally orders Scrap to "just slit these mother*ckers throats and get it over with. I'm tired of looking at these fools." Scrap quickly sliced Junebug's and then Roger's throats.

White Boy grabbed the package that Roger came in with earlier and tossed it to Scrap. "I'll have something else for y'all lter. Finish working his sh*t out the back door then burn this b*tch down." was all Bj said after White Boy finished explaining this morning episode.

"Did you shut the spots down on Hermitage, Wood and Wolcott? 'Cause them boys going to be hot everywhere trying to find out what happened. Ain't no need in no one getting picked up for questioning or popped off with some work. You feel me? " Bj asked.

" I got on top of that as soon as I left Junebug's crib," replied White Boy.

"…and one more thing White Boy,"

"What's that?"

"Send three of our men over to that n*gga crib and shake it down and kill who ever in there. That will send a message to any other n*gga who thinks they can disrespect our land." Bj said.

"Alright bro, I'll hit you on the horn later." White Boy got out and hoped in his car and pulled off.

Bj arrived home, picked up Sheena and Tania and took them to the movie and to Hollywood Park. They had the all you can eat lunch at Old Country Buffet. They made it home around 10:30 that night and Nish was so exhausted that he had to carry her in the house and lay her in her bed. He kissed her on her forehead and yelled for Sheena to come in there and undress Nish and tuck her in.

Sheena and Bj sat in the living room watching the news and

talking about life. His cell phone started vibrating. He didn't pay it any attention until Sheena gave him a look as if she thinks he's trying to hide something, so he looks at the caller ID and then answers it. "White Boy, what's up?"

"Sh*t, everything's taken care of and now we're at the black room watching these hoes shake their ass like a salt shaker. You coming out to kick it or what?" White Boy asks.

"Nah, um, bro, I'm in the crib for the night with my girls."

"Alright, I'm going to holla at you in the A.M. then."

"White Boy, y'all be cool out there and don't get too drunk."

"Ok, I got you big bro, one."

"Aw right, one" and the line went dead.

Bj and Sheena sat cuddled up on the couch till the news went off. They headed towards their bedroom, kissing and touching one another. "Big daddy, what? You trying to start something tonight?" Sheena asks.

"Baby, it's already started," he replies.

She looks down at the bulge in his boxer. "I see somebody trying to break out," she teases.

"Yeah, he can't wait."

When they made it to the room it was on and poppin. They made love and had passionate sex for an hour until they collapses in each other's arms and slept like babies.

Bj, aka Bryant Johnson, was born and raised in the Inglewood neighborhood, which is on the south side of Chicago. He stayed in a home with his mother, Mrs. Barker, his two older brothers and two younger brothers. Mrs. Barker was a strong woman to raise five boys by herself. Well, let's just say that her

15

sons didn't allow any mens living in their home.

Nuke, aka Demarcus Barker, is the oldest, then Lil' Squirrel, aka Willie Johnson Jr., who is one year younger than Bj. They have the same father, Willie Johnson Sr. He was in the Army for 23 years, all the way up till Bj was 15 years old. He was never in their life, until after Lil Squirrel was killed. He popped up at the funeral and tried to convince Bj to come stay in Seattle, Washington. He and Bj had a confrontation about it when Bj told him to go f*ck himself. It was only because of this tragedy that they ever met. This was the first and last time Bj ever saw his father.

Sco, aka Nathan Barker, is the fourth son. He has a different father than his older brothers and also his younger brother. His father was cool but stayed in a separate house than Mrs. Barker. Sco's father passed away when he was seven in a car accident. He had worked at a high maintenance factory, so when he died Sco was left with enough money to take care of him tilll he was 21.

Nardo, aka Lenard Gibson, was the baby boy. His father was the only father figure in any of their lives because he was an O.G. who once lived the street life and was able to adapt and teach them the in's and out's about the streets. He played his part and knew that he didn't call the shots in their household.

After four or five years he went to jail and when he came back home it was to another woman. That was the last straw for a father figure to be apart of their lives. Mrs. Barker made a rule for it to be just her and her boys, well, let's say mens.

Nuke, Bj and Lil Squirrel were some hard core brothers

running through the Englewood area. Anytime you faulted one or had a problem with one, you have a problem with all of them. Mrs. Barker taught them the saying, "that if one fight, all better fight." Bj was the most hard core of them all, because when he was involved in something, someone was definitely going to lose their life or be hurt so bad that they would have wished they were dead, even if it was one of his own family members.

Bj spent three years in the juvenile detention facility for murder when he was 15 years old. He was sentenced to juvenile life in little D.O.C., which means he would have to stay there till he turned 21, but his broyer got him out in three years due to the fact that is was self-defense.

Two guys were jumping on him, but he came out on top and when the police pulled on the scene he was still stumping the guy's head in the ground, after he was already dead. The other guy ran and got away with a busted eye that needed 10 stitches inside and out. The police had to taze him and tackle him just to get in control of the situation.

Bj was 18 when he was released from the juvenile detention facility. He had to take the bus home because his family needed the time to plan his welcome home party to celebrate this early release.

The ride on the bus was boring until after the first stop where they had to pick up some more people. Once the bus came to a complete stop, he sprinted off the bus straight to the place that he loved eating from, McDonald's. After getting his food, he headed back to the bus. As he got closer to the bus he saw movement through the window where he was sitting. He speeds

17

up the steps straight passed the driver, as if something's wrong. The people in the front row seats look at him like he's crazy, as he flies past them heading to the back of the bus.

When he gets to his seat, he sees a female looking out the window. He feels a little at ease that it's not a male but stilll feels the need to say something to get his window seat back.

"Baby girl, that's my seat". She's stilll facing the window, as if she's ignoring him. So, he repeats himself but in an aggressive tone. "Baby girl, that's my seat," stilll she's paying him no attention. He extends his hand to tap her on the shoulder until he sees the cord from the ear plugs hanging past her hair, so he taps the seat instead and she turns around and takes the ear plugs out. Bj stood there with his mouth hanging open as if he can't breathe. He is so mesmerized by this beautiful queen that is sitting in his seat. She has the complexion of the actress Gabriel Union, with the mirror image of Regina King.

She speaks to him, "Hello" and waves her hand to get him out of his trance. But it went in one ear and out the other.

After two seconds, he snaps out of this trance, "I'm sorry I was trying to tell you that you're in my seat, but hey, a brother don't mind sharing with a beautiful lady like yourself." "Excuse me for being rude but my name is Bj."

"Did your mama name you that?" she asks.

"I'm sorry. It's Bryant Johnson, but everybody calls me Bj."

"Well, I prefer to call you Bryant."

"Your wish is my command," he shot back at her.

"Anyways," she said with a slur, "My name is Sheena once again."

18

"Oh, I didn't hear you the first time. Your beauty had me in a trance."

"Yeah, whatever, but are you going to stand up all day or sit down since you have everyone looking at us as if we're movie stars or something."

"Sh*t, the way that old lady over there looking she might think we're terrorists."

Sheena starts laughing and right then and there, Bj knew he had her right where he wanted her.

"So, sheena, you mind telling me where you're from?"

"I'm from Chicago," she replies.

He looks at her and repeats "Chicago" as if he can't believe her.

"Yeah, Chicago," she snaps with a twist of her head with it. "Why is there a problem with that?"

"Whoa, slow down baby girl. Ain't no problem. Don't bite my head off. It's just that I'm from Chicago too, the south side."

"Well, baby boy, I'm from the Village. You do know where that is right?"

"Ain't that like down there by 13th and Ashland or some thing?"

"Yeah and where out south are you from?"

"55th and Woods, well, let's just say a hop, skip and a jump."

"Okayyy," as she drags out the one word reply.

"Bryant, can I ask you where you're coming from, if you don't mind me being nosy?"

He had a look on his face as if he wants to lie, so he won't

19

blow his chance of getting her, but the word came out "Jail". She repeats it.

"Yeah, jail – J.A.I.L. " he spells it out for her.

"I'm not dumb," she snaps.

"I didn't mean it like that baby girl. I was just making a joke."

"Well, it wasn't very funny."

"My fault T."

"My name ain't T, it's Sheena."

"Damn, do you have to be so defensive all the time?"

"I'm sorry your highness. My name is not B, it's Sheena," she repeats in a girl's voice.

"So now you got jokes, huh? But I guess…"

"What, what?"

"That turns me on, sorry boo. This ain't that."

Sheena and Bj went back and forward for the rest of the ride. By the time they reached the downtown bus station, they done got to know each other more and switch info for future use.

Bj flags a cab down and gave him the address to his mother's house. When he arrived out in front of his house, he paid the driver and then exits the cab. He starts looking around as if some thing's not right cause he sees a lot of cars parked on the block. Remembering that he's in the hood and there's never been this many cars around by his neighbors.

He disses the thought from his mind as he remembers that he's been gone for three years and things do change.

He then takes the steps two at a time to get up the long flight of stairs quicker. He reaches for the doorbell but decided to try the door knob first to sneak in and surprise his loved ones. The knob turns and the door comes open, as he enters the house the smell of home cooked foods hits his nose.

The lights in the living room and dining room were out but the light in the kitchen is on, so he knows she's in the kitchen cooking. He closes the door softly and tip toes towards the kitchen to surprise her. As soon as he reached the dining room the lights pop on and people come out from behind the couches, under the table and from behind doors yelling "Surprise"!

His family and friends embraces him with hugs and kisses and welcome home gifts and money. Some of the people he doesn't recognize or even know, but came out anyway to see who is this Bj guy that everyone has been bragging about and waiting for to come home.

Mrs. Barker comes pushing her way through the crowd so she can get her hugs and kisses as well. "Look at my baby. Done gained some weight and is looking all grown and sexy. All these lil gals going to be fighting over you, and boy don't you look just like your daddy?"

"I know ma, I'm looking right at her." Bj always looks at his mom as his daddy cause she is the one who raised him.

He has seen his father one time, so he considers him as just a sperm donor!

"Baby come on in here and eat you some of this home cooked food." his mother says.

"Alright ma, I'll be there in a few. Let me just holla at Nuke for a second," as Bj looks around the room for his big brother. He spots him in the corner with a fine ass female.

"How you doing baby girl?"

"Fine and you?"

"I can't complain. Sh*t, I'm free!"

"That's good, but is you going to stay out?" she said as if she knows him.

"I'm going to try."

"Okay that's good."

"Baby girl do you mind if I steal him from you for a minute?"

"Not at all, just make sure you return him."

"No problem." Bj replied, as he watches her sashay off, but not without giving Bj a sneaky look.

"What's up lil bro?" Nuke asks.

"Nothing, just happy to be free as a bird. You feel me?"

"Hell, yeah! I'm happy that you're home, so you can share this empire I'm building."

"That's what I want to talk to you about."

"Yeah, well let's get our party on tonight and go out to breakfast in the morning and talk then and plus I can show you what I have accomplished since you been gone," Nuke offers.

"Okay, I can dig that" a big bro who was shorty you was over there hugged up on,"" who Meaka, lil bro she ain't sh*t but a jump off, why you like that," she straight. I just never seen her, you want to smash that lil bro,"

"naw I don't want your seconds."

"I'll pass on that one big bro."

"I can make that happen if you want plus she got some bomb ass head."

"Naw, I'm cool right now,"

"Boy, you don't know what you're missing."

"I'll get her one day but right naw, I'm cool right now. My mind is on some dead presidents."

"That's what I'm talking about cause it's a lot of it our here to get."

"We'll see."

"Well lil bro, I'm going to head on out here to the streets and I'll be here in the morning to scoop you up."

"Alright, big bro be safe out there."

Nuke, lifted his shirt up to show his lil brother that he was strapped and said, "I am," as he walked out the door.

Bj mingled around with the rest of the guests until they started leaving. Meaka, who was the fine ass sister who was talking to his brother earlier, was one of the last ones to leave as she was hoping she didn't have to leave and be the first one to try to lock Bj down with the bomb ass head that all the ballers tells her she has, but he already made his mind up that he would be sleeping alone, peacefully, tonight. As he let everyone out and locked the door behind them.

He walked in the kitchen to get him some food to eat cause his stomack was doing flips. His mother was in there cleaning up and putting things away, as he approached the kitchen.

"Ma, you can go on in there and get some rest. I know you been on your feet all day. I'll just fix me something to eat and then finish cleaning up the place."

She gave him a look and said," You think you're going to push me away when I haven't gotten my time in. Child, please!

You better fix your plate and sit down and listen to what I have to say."

After fixing his plate and sitting down at the table, his mother pulled her a chair up right across from him to start her lecture that she'd been waiting all night to deliver.

"So what are your plans now that you're home?"

"Well Ma, Nuke going to take me to go get my state ID in the morning and then I'm going to go fill out some job application."

"That's good cause I hope you're not going to get out there like your brother cause all he want and care about is them streets and corners that he thinks he is running. I try to talk to him but he don't listen, so I just pray for him and put it in good hands."

"Mom, don't worry yourself to death about him. He going to be alright."

"I hope so."

"He will. Trust me, plus he's grown now."

"You're right baby. I just don't want you to get in any more trouble."

"I'm not Ma. When do Nat come home from school?

"He should be home next month for good. Well, the summer I mean cause he's taking his tail back in September. He got 3 more years to get his bachelor degree as a paralegal and I'm so proud of him."

"Yeah, me too, Ma."

Nardo is over at your grandmother's house cause him and your Auntie Angie's son Ben be going to school together. So he goes over there before it gets too late. "Yeah, Ma how is

Grandma doing?"

"They're fine. Your Grandma still going to the boat every week and playing cards every Friday."

"Ma, all that gambling she do she should be rich by now. She will one day or at least die trying."

"Well, I'm going to go on in here and get me some rest cause I have to be at Mrs. Betty's house at 11:00 in the morning."

"Mrs. Betty! Ma, who is that?"

"She is one of the old ladies that I do home care for five times a week."

"Oh, well I'll see you in the morning before you leave then."

"Okay baby good night and make sure you don't leave the lights on cause my bills are already high."

"Okay, old lady," he jokes.

"I got your 'old lady', alright," she chides back. "Good night baby."

Bj just finished eating and cleaned up the kitchen and was heading towards the dining room to straighten it up until he heard a knock on the door. At first he thought he was hearing things, until the knock came again. He walked to the door to look through the peep hole.

He sees Meaka and wonders what could be wrong. He opens the door to ask what is wrong. "I think I have a nail stuck in my tire or something cause it's a flat and I don't have a spare time." "So I was hoping that you can use your mother's car and give me a ride home?"

"Why didn't you call a cab?"

"Well, cabs don't come around here this time of the night."

"You mean to tell me that there's no one you can call to come pick you up?"

"I tried everyone but no one is answering their phone."

"Step in Meaka and let me see if my mother is still awake." He goes to her door and can hear her snoring, so he crosses that thought out of his mind. "Well, she's sleep, but if you want to crash on the couch for tonight you can. "

"That would be OK if it's not a problem."

"There's no problem."

"Thank you, Bj. I really appreciate this."

"Well, as you can see I'm cleaning up in here, so you can go sit in the kitchen until I finish up in here."

"If you don't mind, the least I can do is help you."

"Sure, that will be Okay. You can get the dining rom and I'll get in here."

Bj and Meaka went to work cleaning up the living room and dining room. While doing so, Meaka got her feel on every chance she can get, cause this was the plan that she sat in her car and came up with and so far its working.

After they finished cleaning up, they sat in the living room watching TV and also making small talk until he decided to call it a night. He gets up and goes to the closet and returns with a pillow and blanket for Meaka and then heads to his room to lay it down.

While laying in the bed daydreaming for an hour, thinking

did Meaka do this on purpose to try and sleep with him. He hears a tap on the door. He ignores it the first time, then the tap came again and the door comes open. Meaka peeks her head in and call his name.

"What's the problem now Meaka?"

"Can you show me where the bathroom is?"

As he gets out of the bed with only his boxers on she stares at his body for a minute. "The bathroom is not in here. It's this way."

He shows her where the bathroom is then goes back to his room. He starts to put the lock on the door but decides not to. He wants to see if she's going to try and sneak back in.

Ten minutes later, she's at his door again. This time she comes in without knocking and walks over to the bed to join him. He stops here and asks "What is you doing?"

"Can I lay in here with you? We don't have to do anything."

"What is something wrong with sleeping on the couch or your whole plan was to try and sleep with me tonight?"

"What if it was?"

"Well, all you had to do is come right out and say what you wanted."

"Yeah, well I want to get f*cked and you is my pick."

"Since you so bold with it, I just want some head."

"Oh, I'm a professional at that too."

She pulls her shirt over her head and unsnaps her bra then tosses it on the floor. Her 34 c size breast sit up as if she stilll has her bra on. Bj massages his piece as he watches her put on a strip tease. She now knows she got him right where she wants him, as she takes her time peeling off her jeans. Bj can't help his self anymore, so he walks over to help her out of her jeans. He pushes her on the bed and pulls them off from her knees. He then pulls her thong down but before he can get them pass her knees, she moves his hand and pulls them back up. "There's no need for them to come off sweetie," she whispers. "I thought you only wanted some head."

"I do."

"Well, daddy, you need to be taking your boxers off, not mine."

"You ain't said nothing but a word," as he snatches his boxers off in 0.2 seconds.

She sees the size of his penis and smiles.

She reaches and grabs his piece and starts jerking him off until he stops her. "Lil mama, I did enough of that where I just came from."

She then leans her head forward and starts licking the tip, then the side and back up to the tip. "Now, that's what I'm, talking about!"

She then sucks on the head and jiggles his balls at the same time. He lets out a soft moan, as she continues to teas the head. She then goes down further and further until all 10 inches is not to be seen. She comes up a little then back down as she makes humming noises. "Oh, sh*t...girl. Oh yeah, just like that...He reaches to palm her head but she knocks his hand away. She then comes half way up and then back down in a fast motion and stays down there for a few seconds while stilll humming. He jerks a little and now she knows she has got him right where she wants him. She goes in for the kill, as she goes up and down in a faster motion. "Ooh sh*t girl! I'm cumin'!. Ooh yeah! You gonna catch that sh*t girl? Yeah, catch that sh*t, ooh, here it come girl! Yeah, catch that sh*t! Here it cum. Swallow all of it...ooh, ooh, ooh sh*t!" he says as he shot the last of it down her throat. He tried to pull away, but she wasn't having that, as she kept sucking on him and jerking on him faster, so he wouldn't go limp. At this point, he's going crazy now. He can barely talk as she goes to work. He pushes her head off him and says, "I want to f*ck the sh*t out of you."

"I see you changed your mind, huh?"

"Just take them thongs off, girl."

"Naw, boo, you take them off," she says as she leans back and lifts her legs in the air. Instead of pulling them off, he rips them off instead.

She spreads her legs wide open and starts playing with her shaved p*ssy. He gets extra excited at the site and climbs on top of her and enters her wet cave. She moans and moans as he strokes in and out slowly. "Oh yeah, daddy I want you to f*ck me harder daddy."

She's squirming up and down cause he's only putting the head in and out as she begs for more. "Daddy take this p*ssy. Daddy it's yours, daddy." He then plunges all the way in and back out slow. "Ooh, sh*t daddy, yeah, yeah, harder daddy. Tear this p*ssy up, yeah like that! Oh yes, daddy, oh yeah, mmm, mmm, yeah daddy. It's in my stomach. Daddy, ooh, oh, ah, ah, ah, daddy keep coming faster! Don't stop daddy!" Bj is ramming her like crazy now. She cums all over his d*ck. He pulls out fast and she jumps.

"Turn that ass around so I can hit it from the back."

She can barely turn around cause she's stilll shaking from the orgasm she just had. He flips her over and enters her from the back. Her ass is shaking up and down with every stroke. He starts slapping her ass as he tries to punish her. "Ooh, sh*t baby."

"Oh, yes daddy, punish this p*ssy, daddy. Oh, yeah daddy, put it in my ass. Daddy, please!"

"You want it in the ass, huh?"

"Oh, yeah, daddy!"

He continues to bang her p*ssy, as he finger f*cks her ass.

"Oh, wee daddy, I'm cumming again. Daddy, oh sh*t daddy, yeah daddy, like that daddy. Harder, harder daddy!"

"You love this d*ck don't you?"

"Ooh, yeah, daddy. I love this d*ck daddy, cum with me! Daddy, yeah daddy. I'm cumming daddy!"

He feels his nut cumming and starts long stroking her harder.

"Ooh, sh*t daddy!. I'm cummingg!" she moans.

He pulls out and shoots his semen all over her butt and back, as she falls on her stomach, while shaking from her own orgasm.

"Damn, girl! You got some good ass p*ssy!"

"I know and you almost missed out on your shot trying to play hard to get. Stay like that and don't get that sh*t on my sheets while I go get you a towel."

Bj wakes up from three loud knocks that Nuke gave to the

bedroom door, as if he was trying to knock the hinges off.

"Who that?" Bj yells.

"It's me N*gga! Open the door!" shouts Nuke.

"Hold on N*gga. I'll be down there in a minute, " Bj shoots back.

"Hurry up N*gga. We ain't got all day. I told you that I'd be here bright and early and plus you should be used to getting up early in the morning from where you just came from."

"N*gga, f*ck you. I told you I'll be down in a minute."

"Meaka, get up girl. We got to be out. You want me to call you a cab or something?" Bj asks.

"How am I going to be able to get my car fixed?"

"Oh, sh*t I forgot all about your car. Let me go down here and ask my bro to take me to get your tire fixed. I should let you do it yourself for being slick for a dick, you put your own car on a flat."

"Boy, please, you wasn't saying that when I had your dick all down my throat was you?"

"Hell, naw and you wasn't saying anything when I was all up in your stomach either."

"Sh*t I want you to put it back in my stomach now to wake me up fully."

"Naw, we ain't on that. I got things to do this morning."

"Well, just let me suck it."

"Girl, you something else. What you're a nimpho or something?"

"I just like good dick."

31

"Girl, I'll be back. Just put your clothes on."

"And if I don't?"

"You're going to be leaving out of here naked and riding home on a flat tire."

"You wouldn't do that, would you?"

As he was leaving out the door, he turned around and told her, "Don't try me," and closed the door.

As he walks into the kitchen, where his mother was over the stove cooking breakfast and talking to his brother at the same time, the phone started ringing.

"Baby, can you go in there and answer the phone?" she asks.

Bj ran to catch it before it stops ringing.

"Hello."

"Can I speak to Mrs. Barker, please?" the caller asks.

"May I ask who's calling?" Bj responds.

"This is Miss Betty."

"Can you hold for a second?"

"Sure."

"Mom, Miss Betty on the phone for you."

"I'm coming. Tell her to hold on," mom shoots back.

Bj sets the phone down and walks back towards the kitchen. Mrs. Barker walks past him then yells over her shoulder, "Bryant, don't let me food burn."

"Okay, mom."

He walks into the kitchen and gives his brother some dap before going to the stove.

"What's up big bro?"

"Nothing lil' homie. Waiting for your ass."

"Ain't that Meaka's car out front?"

"Hell, yeah."

"Oh, sh*t. I bet you crushed that sh*t , huh?"

"It was alright, but the head was off the chain."

"I told you so."

"She still upstairs in the room lil bro?"

"Hell, yeah."

"Sh*t, let me go up there and get me some head right quick."

"Naw, n*gga. We ain't on that."

"Don't tell me you're sprung on that sh*t already?"

"Hell, naw."

Mrs. Barker walks in and slaps Bj in the back of his head and tell him, "Boy, you better watch your mouth up in my house."

"I'm sorry ma, I thought you was still on the phone."

"Naw, I heard y'all up in here talking about some gal."

"Nuke I need you to take me to get her tire fixed. It's on a flat." Bj said.

"Well, she put it on a flat just to spend a night. That girl is crazy

"I know you ain't got no skeezer up in my house boy?"

"Stella, why you eaves dropping?" Bj asks.

"Well you should know how to whisper then and you won't have to worry about me being nosy." Mom quips.

"Well, yes I have a friend upstairs. Can she stay in there until I get back from getting her tire fixed? I'm not taking you lil bro unless she's paying me." Bj said.

"Boy, please," Mrs. Barker continues. "All you think about is money."

Nuke starts singing, "Money, money, money, money, money. Boy shut your crazy self-up. He can take my car."

"I'm just playing lil bro. let's ride so we can go handle our business."

"What boy?" Mrs. Barker yells. "I mean what business!"

"Bryant don't let your brother get you out there in them no good streets."

"Ma, he's just trying to get under your skin."

"Alright boy, remember what I told you last night. You go to them streets you're going to be living on them streets."

"Ma, I'm going to get my ID and fill out some job applications, not no streets." Bj reassures her.

"Alright boy, as long as you heard what I said."

"Let's ride big bro. I don't know why you always getting her started."

"Bryant before you leave, go upstairs and tell that gal to come down here and get some of this food. I know she hungry after all that noise y'all was making last night." Mrs. Barker insists.

"Ma, please…"

When Bj and Nuke returned from getting the tire fixed, Mrs. Barker and Meaka were sitting at the kitchen table talking.

"What's up Meaka?" Nuke said with a smile on his face.

"Nuke, don't start, please." Meaka said with an embarrassed

34

look on her face (to be in front of 2 brothers that she's been sleeping with).

"Hey, don't look like that. I'm not mad at you. Just keep it in the family."

Mrs. Barker gave him a look as if she would kill him if he say one more disrespectful word towards Meaka. He took that as a sign to drop the suBject. "Well, let's head out of here and go get your business done this morning, while it's still early."

Bj and Nuke were on their way back from the Secretary of State's office where Bj got his driver license and state ID. As the rode around through the neighborhoods on the south side, Nuke was pointing out all of his territory and also his enemy territory.

While driving through 58th and Throop, there was about 20 guys in the middle of the block with blue and black cloths on, which lets you know that their gangstas. This part of the hood calls their set "No Love City."

"A lil bro, you see that light skin cat right there leaning up against that red Cadillac truck?"

"Yeah, I see him and that truck. It looks right too."
"Yeah, I know. His name is Tear Drop. He's a smooth cat. He calls the shots from Loomis to Halsted, which is about a 30 block radius. He's also one of my top customers too. He and the cops have a peace treaty, but you know it's getting hot and N*ggas going to start acting a fool. So, I'm 'bout to put something in motion in the next 2 weeks."

Nuke and Bj rode around making small talk and coming up with plans to expand their territory. "A lil bro, we have the nationwide picnic coming up next week and it's going to be off the chain, plus, I'm going to show you your crew cause I want you to control the muscle."

"I don't know Big bro. I'm planning on sitting back for a few months on some light sh*t cause the po-pos going to be waiting on a n*gga to slip up so they can try to throw away the key this time."

"Come on, lil bro, you the only one I can trust to watch my back and not try to snake me in the end."

"Lets just take it one day at a time big bro. "

"I need to know by next week cause I got this big move in 2 weeks and I'm going to need you."

"OK, big bro. Count me in but I need to play a low key profile."

:"Thanks, lil bro, I need you and you're not going to regret this. Lets stop at my crib. I got a surprise for you."

Nuke and Bj pulled into the 6 car garage that Nike owned out in Country Club Hills. "Damn big bro, all these your rides? Bj asks.

"Yeah, every one of them."

"You're doing it like that?"

"I'm trying to, but hey, what good is it if I can't share it with my lil bro?"

"Come on now, you know I can't ride around in one them expensive cars and I just got out less than 24 hours ago. The po-pos will be all on me before I can get my feet wet."

"Come in here, so I can show you how I'm living."

Bj and Nuke got on the built in elevator from the garage and got off on the first floor. As they stepped off the elevator, Bj thought he was in a famous person's home or something. The living room was all white marble floors and even the tables were marble. In the center of the room was spiral stairs that went all the way up to the third floor. "Damn, big bro! This is a big ass crib just for you and Tiff." Bj exclaimed.

Tiffany is Nuke's wife, who is pregnant with twin boys. She has been with him from when he didn't have a dime. In fact, the way he got on was cause she gave him $3,000 of the $4,800 she got back from her income tax refund and he never looked back.

"We'll be adding three more to this house hold."

"What you mean?" Bj asks.

"Well, Tiff is pregnant with twins, which makes two and I'm giving you the whole second floor," Nuke explains.

"Come on now you know I can't leave Ma that quick and plus you and Tiff gone need some privacy,"

"Come on lil bro. That's why I bought this big ass house. Come up here and check the second floor out. I bet you change your mind then."

Nuje and Bj take the stairs to the second floor, which has a door that leads to a personal apartment of its own. The second floor has its own kitchen, dining and living rooms. The king size bedroom has a Jacuzzi in the middle of the room. "Lil bro, you mean to tell me that you don't want to stay here?" Nuke asks.

"It ain't that. It's just Ma, You know what she's goin to think if I just move out 2 days after I come home. I can't put that pressure on her."

"You right lil bro. Just remember it's yours whenever you ready."

"I got you big bro and thanks a lot."

"Don't thank me, lil n*gga. What's mine is your. Well, since you don't want this apartment, I know you're not going to turn down what's in that top draw over there."

"What's in there?"

"Look over there and see, if I tell you then I shouldn't put it in there."

Bj walked over and opened the drawer. "Damn, big bro, all this for me?"

"Yeah, all of it."

Bj starts pulling stacks and stacks out of the draw. "What's this about 20 G's?"

"Naw, lil bro, double that and a half. 50 G's."

"You bull sh*tting!"

"Count it!"

"Naw, I believe you."

""So, what you gonna do with that little change you got?"

"I'm gone take five and get me a car and…" "Hold up lil bro, I got six cars downstairs that you can drive since you won't let me give you one."

"I already told you the situation about the car thang, so I'm gone buy a low key car until next year."

"OK, sh*t it's your money. Do what you want to do but remember one thing…"

"What's that big bro?"

"Make it grow!"

"I am after I buy me like $5,000 worth of shoes and clothes."

"Ain't no need for that either. Go look in the double door closet over there."

Bj opened the closet to about 30 different name brand outfits hanging neatly in the closet with at least 20 pair of sneakers to go with them. "Thanks a lot big bro, I owe you big time."

"Naw, you don't owe me sh*t, but your loyalty."

"I will always be loyal to you even if we was broke."

"That's love lil bro."

Bj pulled out the paint shop in this 1993 Cutlass sitting on 19" assassin with a 9" TV in both sun visors. He had paid $2500 for the candy apple red paint job with gold glitter in it and now heading to the sound shop to put four 12" speakers in his trunk so you can hear him four blocks away.

After leaving the sound shop, Bj was riding around enjoying his sounds when he was pulled over for his radio being too loud.

"Excuse me sir, can you step out the car and keep your hands where I can see them?"

"What seems to be the problem officer?"

"I said 'step out the muther f*cking car and put your hands where I can see them.'"

"Officer I have license and insurance if you want to see them, but there''s no reason for me to get out my car."

"Oh, I see we have a smart ass here."

"Sir, I'm not being smart. I'm just following the bro."

"Well, if you were following the bro, you wouldn't have your sounds up loud."

"I apologize for that."

"Well, hand me over your license and registration and keep your hands on the wheel where I can see them, so we don't have no accident." Bj did as he was told.

Ten minutes pass and the officer still hasn't returned with his license and registration. "What the f*ck's taking so long? I hope they not on no bullsh*t." Three more minutes has passed, then the officer returns to the car.

"Say Mr. Johnson, where do I know you from?"

"Sir, you don't know me."

"You sure cause your name rings a bell, but I can't put my finger on it. Here's your registration and I'm not going to write you a ticket but keep the music down."

"Thank you, sir."

Bj pulled off and was looking in the rearview mirror at the officer who stood there watching his car until he truned the corner.

Bj was in his room putting on his clothes to attend the nationwide picnic. So far his day has been going fine all morning, except for the run in with the bro, but he brushed that off his shoulders.

While putting on some cologne and sizing himself in the mirror, his phone started vibrating. He looked at the caller ID and saw Sheena's name and number. He answers the phone, "Well how are you doing today, beautiful?" "Fine."

"And what do I owe you to be talking so sweet today? What

a brother can't be happy to hear from his soon o be girlfriend?"

"How do you know I want you to be my man?"

"Because who wouldn't?"

"Don't flatter yourself, Bryant."

"Well, what did I do to get this call today? I haven't heard from you since we went out the day before yesterday."

"Well, that's why I'm calling you to let you know that I had a good time and I was wondering if we can go out to the movies or something, my treat."

"Ain't that so sweet? You want to treat your man to the movie."

"Don't say it like I'm cheap or something and you're not my man. We're just friends."

"Well, what if I don't want to go to …"

Before he can finish, Sheena interrupts, "Well, you don't have to go out with me then."

"Hold on baby, you snapping on a brother and won't even let me finish."

"Cause you saying it like I got to kiss your ass for you to go out with me."

"Slow down, damn!" he said in a demanding voice. "I was trying to ask you to go to this picnic with me instead of the movie, but your attitude is telling me you don't want to go. You want to have it your way."

"I'm sorry Bryant. I would love to go with you."

"Don't be sorry, be nice," he jokes.

"Don't push it boy!"

"I got your boy."

"Well, let me finish getting dressed and I'll be at your crib in 30 minutes."

"Alright and once again, I'm sorry."

"Don't do that girl. I kind of like your attitude. I tell you it turns me on."

"Boy, just call me when you are on your way. Bye."

"Alright, bye."

Bj and Sheena were riding through the forest preserve where the picnic was being held, listening to John B. "Don't listen to what people say. They don't know about, bout you and me. Put it out your mind, cause its jealousy. They don't know about this."

Everybody and their mama was there and all the attention was on his ride and the sounds cause it sounded so clear, even with all the bass it was pushing out.

As they pulled up to a parking space that had a sign that read, "Reserved for Bj only!" He knew he was at the right spot. He parked and got out and came around to the passenger side to let Sheena out of the car. As she got out, all eyes were on her. She was wearing a beige Baby Phat halter top and beige capris with some open toe stillettos to match.

As they made their grand entrance, they were approached by two bouncers with "Security" on their shirts. "Nice to meet you boss. We was assigned as your body guards by your big brother."

"With all due respect, I'm cool. Just tell him I sent y'all

away."

"Boss, we was given orders and our lives are on the line if we don't follow them."

"Well, I just gave y'all an order and I advise y'all to follow it."

"Bryant, would you just let them do what they was told." Sheena asked.

"Sheena, please speak when you're spoken to!"

She left the subject alone as she saw the look in Bj's eye, showing that he wasn't comfortable with what was going on. Bj sees Nuke coming toward him with 3 security as well.

"What's up lil bro? Looks like you're not in a good mood right now."

"Well I was until these security guards you sent can't listen. Sh*t was about to get ugly." Bj responds.

"Calm down lil bro. I gave them the order."

"Well when I gave them an order to push on, they should have took my order and since they didn't, you better fire their asses cause when you gave them the word that I'm their boss then from that point on my orders were the only ones they follow. They failed the test, big bro."

"Hey Big Rock and Big Bo, y'all go over there and keep a eye on our rides. I'm going to give y'all another job," Nuke says.

The 2 security did as they was told and Nuke called on 2 more security to fall in place. "I like the ride, Lil bro. Sh*t ain't f*cking with your sh*t."

" What's that, a Camaro?" Bj asks.

43

"Naw, Lil bro, that's next year's Viper. I had it shipped from overseas. They only made five of them and that's the second one that was made."

"Lil bro, who is my Lil Sister that you're with?"

"Oh, my fault. This is Sheena. I met her on the bus when I came home. I'm trying to get her to be my girl, but she's playing hard to get," Bj offers as Sheena punches him in his arm.

Nuke pulled out a wad of money and said, "Nice to meet you, Sheena. How much will it cost for you to be my brother's girlfriend? You know I try to give him whatever he want."

She responds by saying, "Well, let me see…Your life if you disrespect me again!"

"Hold on, Lil Sis. It was just a joke."

"Lil bro, you better keep her. You got a winner and one with heart at that!"

"Yeah, Big bro, I'm feeling her," Bj beams.

"Let's go over here and get some of this food. This picnic cost me almost 20 grand."

"I see Big bro, you just spend money like its raining money."

"Naw, Lil bro, you got to give back and enjoy it at the same time."

"I feel ya."

"Let me take you over here and introduce you to your team and some big players in my committee. Hey, Tiff come here for a second." Nuke's wife comes over as she was called. She's four months pregnant and you can't even tell. "Nuke continues, "Tiff, this is Bj's girl, Sheena."

"Hi, how are you doing, Tiff?" Sheena asks.

"Hi, how are you Sheena?" Tiff asks.

"Bay, I want you to keep her company while me and Bj talk to a few people," Nuke explained.

"Alright bay."

"Hey Tag and Rob y'all try to keep a tight guard on them, as if y'all lives depend on it," Nuke requests of 2 security nearby.

"Alright boss," they reply. Nuke and Bj went one way and the rest went the other way.

The first group of people they walked up to had Terror Town on their shirt (which lets you know what set they're from). Tony Red is the Prince of them, so he is the man I want to talk to.

"What's up T. Red? How's everything been going?" Nuke asks.

"I can't complain, except I wish I had your hand."

"Aye, what's mine is yours!"

"I feel you, by the way I appreciate you bringing all the brothers together today."

"This is nothing. I'm trying to put something together so that we can do this more than once a year," Nuke replies.

"I know right!"

"T. Red I want you to meet my lil bro, Bj."

"What's up Bj? It's an honor to finally meet you. Everyone been talking about you, homie," T. Red says.

"Yeah, I'm glad to be out of that rat hole. Sh*t, I wouldn't wish that on my worst enemy," Bj replies.

"Aye, T. Red, I'm trying to expand my area a lot farther and I put my lil bro in charge of the muscle, so I was hoping that you can send some of your trusted hard core brothers to join his team so we can take over No Love City. And once we take it over, I'm willing to give you three blocks to do what ever you want," Nuke offers.

"That sounds good Nuke. I'll send ten of my mans to you tomorrow and if you need anything else, just hit my number."

"I will T. Red. Gratitude for your hand."

"That's nothing, one hand washes the other."

"No doubt! Let me get over here and catch me one of these honey's to take with me and Bj here, welcome home." T. Red tossed him a rubber band full of hundreds. "Thanks, brother!"

Nuke and Bj went around the park meeting and discussing their plans with Prince Ron from Ducktown, Prince RJ from Rack City, Prince Tone-Tone from Foster Park, Prince Paco from Crank Town, Prince Bo Bo from Stone Tez and a few more sets and came out with good response from all of them and after tomorrow, they would be able to put their plan in effect.

Nuke and Bj finished the rest of the day chit-chatting and watching the workers clean up before it was time to leave.

"Aye Big bro, me and Sheena about to catch the last show at Evergreen Plaza. You and Tiff want to come?"

"Naw, lil bro, go head and enjoy yourself and if you don't want to go to mom's house, call my phone when you're on your way."

"Alright, Big bro. Drive safe."

"Tiff will. I'm riding shotgun."

"OK."

Bj and Sheena sat in the theater cuddled up during the whole move like couples. After it was over he offered for her to drive home while he lay back in the passenger seat. She was all for it.

"Bryant, I want you to know that I had a nice time today."

"I did too as well. Sheena, can I ask you a question?"

"Anything Bryant."

"Why is it that you don't want to let m be your man?"

"Bryant, I like you a lot already' but I don't want to let my guards down to get hurt," she explains.

"I don't want to hurt you Sheena. I want to learn how to love you in every way possible."

"I've been told that before and got hurt in the end."

"Sheena, you're stilll young like me and you can't let one relationship keep you out of the next one. You're going to have problems in life, but you have to take chances and still getting our feelings hurt in the end I can't speak about your past, but I'm here to love your feelings. Just give me a chance," as he leaned over and planted a soft kiss on her lips and she didn't resist. Instead she took it further with a French kiss. They kissed passionately for what seemed like forever.

"Bryant, can I spend the night with you tonight?"

"Sure you can. I thought you would never ask!"

Bj gave her the direction to his apartment on the way to his house he called to let his Big brother know he was on the way. As they ride home, he called to let his mother know that he was going to spend the night out, so she wouldn't be worried.

Sheena and Bj pulled up in the driveway. "Where we parking at, in the garage?"

"No, just pull up a lil bit more and kill the engine. We have to park out here cause my brother got all them cars in the garage,

47

like he need all of them."

"Is this his house?"

"Yeah, he got the first and third floors and I got the second floor. It's 3 different floors in this house. We just going to go o my floor and tomorrow when everybody's woke, I'll show you the whole place."

""Alright, you want me to grab your bags out of the back seat?"

"Naw, I got it."

"Here you can open the garage door though, while I get the bags." He tossed her the door keys, then reached in the back seat and grabbed the bags.

As they enter the garage, Sheena was so mesmerized at all the luxury cars. "These are y'all cars?" she asks.

"No, them his cars. I wouldn't waste my money on six cars that I can't drive."

"That's right, but hey, you only live once. so why not enjoy it."

"I can enjoy two luxury cars, but six is too much."

"I like that Porsche. That's every girls dream car."

"One day I might buy you one."

"For real?"

"Yeah girl, I'm for real, but we have to be settled down then."

"As long as you treat me right, then I'm all yours forever," Sheena smiled as she pushed the middle button on the elevator. "An elevator in this house?"

"Yeah, I told him he should sign up for 'Cribs'."

Bj and Sheena got off on the second floor and exited the elevator, which starts right at the spiral stairs that lead to the first floor going down and the third floor going up.

"Ooh, I love this house already and I haven't even seen the rest of it!"

"Come on in here Boo. I'll show you the rest tomorrow, like I promised."

As they enter the apartment, Bj was shocked at the scene before him. Nuke had Tiff to make it look so romantic. She had lit candles, trailing towards the Jacuzzi to make it look like a walkway. She also had candles around the Jacuzzi and an ice bucket with a bottle of champagne and two glasses sitting on the edge of the spa.

"Oh, Bryant, I feel so special!"

He came up with a quick lie, "Yeah, we have to thank Tiff for taking the time to make this a special night for us. No need in spoiling the moment." Bj said as he started getting undressed.

"Bryant, I don't have on no bikini, but I guess my bra and panty will help." She got undressed and Bj helped her up the steps to the Jacuzzi.

The bedroom was dark except for the candles lit throughout the room. "Bj grabbed the remote and pressed play and Excape came blasting through the stereo, "Do you want to like I want,, to be in love with you, say you do…"

Sheena scooted closer to Bj and started nibbling on his ear and kidding on his neck. They kissed and fondled with each other until Sheena got hot as a fire

49

cracker. She stood up and reached for his hand to guide him towards the king sized bed. As she walked down the Jacuzzi stairs he grabbed a towel and wrapped it around her and dried her off as she walked towards the bed. He couldn't help but watch her perfectly round shaped ass as it jiggled in a rhythmic motion as she walked.

She stopped by the bed and turned around and grabbed the towel, so she can dry him off as well. After she finished drying him off, he leaned his body into hers, so that they both can collapse on the bed. He kissed her soft lips, then around her neck and down to her breast. She lifted up so he can take her bra off, so he can have his way. She moaned as he went back and forward from one breast to the other and down to her navel. She moaned out in pleasure. He pulled at her panties. She arched her hips up to make it easier for him to pull them off. Once he got them off he went back to her treasure chest and started playing with her pearl tongue.

"Oh, yes, Bryant, I'm about to cumm…"

He started moving his finger in and out faster and faster' while still sucking her tongue, as if it's a Now & Later.

"Oooh, yes, baby, ooh, ooh, aah, boyyby," she yelled as she came all over his face. He continued fingering her in the same pace as she moan and begged for him to enter the womb. "Ooh sh*t baby, I want you inside me, Onh, sh*t baby, ooh, ooh, aah, babay, please baby. I can't take it anymore. Bryant, I'm cumming! Oh sh*t, oh yeah, right there baby, ooh, ooh," she started shaking out of control as she had her second orgasm.

He came up and kissed her on the lips while he positioned

himself between her legs and entered her slowly. She was super tight, but her juices helped him get all the way in without hurting her. She moaned even louder every time he made it all the way inside of her.

"Ooh, yes baby, you like this dick?"

"I love this dick baby." "Ah sh*t daddy, harder daddy. This is your p*ssy Daddy. Ooh, ooh, uh, uh daddy. I'm cuming Daddy. Yes, Daddy you're hitting my spot Daddy," as she started shaking and jerking as she came like Niagara Falls.

Bj rolled her over on top of him without even pulling out of her. She took her position, as her turn to give him a ride of a life time. As she got into the dog position. she moved her body in a rhythm as if she had a hula hoop on her waist. Bj moaned out in pleasure while Sheena moaned even louder. She rode him for what seemed like a life time, until he felt like he only had twenty seconds left. He flipped her over in the doggy style, so he can lay his foundation down. He palmed her soft ass cheeks, while ramming her as if he was trying to break some thing.

Sheena cried out in pain, but it didn't sopt her from asking for more. He pulled out slowly and smacked her ass to watch it shake then plunged back in real fast.

"Oh, sh*t daddy. You trying to.. ooh, daddy, I'm cumming..." were the only words she could drag as she tried to get them fully out.

Bj started pumping faster and faster as he felt himself ready to explode as well. He thought about pulling out, but it felt so good that he didn't stop. While she was shaking, as she let her load out, he pushed every drop of his load inside her. He collapsed on top of her breathing out of control, while still inside her.

Sheena laid on his chest thinking about their future while making circular movement with her finger around the lining of his six pack.

"What you're thinking about?" Bj asked.

"Us and where we go from here," she replied.

"We can't go nowhere but forward unless you got other places."

"Bryant, I just don't want to be hurt again."

""Sheena, I'm feeling you as much as you're feeling me, if not more. I have feelings to, so let's not hurt each other."

"Bryan, there's one thing I have to tell you."

"What's that?"

"I have a daughter already and her name is Tania and she's three years old."

"Well, that means we have a daughter. I love a package deal," as he kissed her on the forehead. They talked a lil longer before they went to sleep.

Bj opened the curtains to let the sun light shine on Sheena's beautiful face as she slept like an angel. He walked over to the bed with a silver platter in his hand that held the breakfast that Tiff had been cooking all morning. "Rise and shine, my nude queen," he said as one of her breasts were exposed.

"Can you please get that sun out of my face and what time is it?" she said as she pulled the sheet over her head.

"Girl, you better get up and eat this breakfast, while its still hot and I know you're hungry after al that love making we did

52

last night."

"Boy, pass me that food with your crazy self."

After Sheena finished eating Tiff gave her a tour of the house while Nuke and Bj sat in the private room conversating about today's event.

"Ring, ring, ring…" Nuke's cell phone started ringing.

"Hello, what's up, Nuke?" the caller on the other end of the phone said, "Just sitting here talking to my lil bro, but I'll be where you're at in an hour," Nuke replied.

"OK, I'll be waiting for you. One" and the line went dead.

"Everything's cool, big bro?" Bj asked.

"Yeah, everything's gravy. I know you got to take your girl home, so gone get on top of that and call my phone when you leave from in front of her house, so I can tell you my location. So we can get our plans on the road."

"Awight, big bro. Give me like 40 minutes."

When Bj walked in the kitchen Sheena and Tiff was in a girls conversation. "Sorry to interrupt y'all gossip, but sweetheart we need to be rolling," he stated.

"Alright, give me a minute, Bay," Sheena said as she got up and headed up the stairs to get her purse and things. When she came back down, she gave Tiff a hug and said her goodbyes and headed for the door. As she made it to the garage, she sees Bj's car parked in the garage, but he's not in it. She turns to go back in the house to look for him, but he blows the Lexus's horn. He lets the window down.

"I'm over here, Sheena," he shouted. She got in and they pull off.

53

Bj pulled in front of her house and parked. "So, when will I see you again?" Sheena asks.

"I want it to be every night, but maybe it's too early to be asking you to move in?" he replies.

"Huh? I was thinking the same thing, but maybe we need to wait a couple of months, so I can get things right with my mother and daughter."

"Will I be able to get you tonight?"

"You know I have to be at work at ten tomorrow."
"Well, you should bring your work clothes with you. "Cause I'm coming to get you~"

"I see some body's demanding already."

"You told me that you was mine last night, so I'm trying to keep it like that."

"Boy, we was having sex when I said that."

"Well, tonight, I'm going to punish that thang so it can play when we're not having sex."

"I'm sorry."

"Don't' suck up now, it's on."

"Bryant, call me when you're on your way."

He gave her a kiss and told her it would be around ten or eleven and she exited the car. He waited till she got in the house before he pulled off of his way to meet Nuke.

Bj hit Nuke on the phone as he rode up 55th and Ashland looking for his brother's car. "Yo, where you at, 'cause I don't see your car."

"I'm in the beauty shop with Sam. I parked my caron Marshfield."

"Okay, I'm about to park and come in."

"Naw, lil bro, pull around the back and park in back of the shop. The back door is always open."

When Bj made it in Sam was laying on his weight bench repping 225 like it wasn't heavy. The old man was standing in position to spot him if he needed help while Nuke was doing curls with the 50 pound dumb bells.

"How you brothers doing?" Bj asked.

"Well," they said in unison.

"Who the last man. so I can show y'all how it's done?"

The old man who is the Prince of C-wop City spoke up, "I'm last and you can fall in after me. This is only the third set, so you have to play catch up."

"No problem. What is it 15 a set?"

"Naw, 10 a set, we ain't trying to burn out."

"OK, I'll do 20 to catch up then."

Sam, who is the old man's right hand man spoke up, "So, what's the plan you got going Nuke?"

"Now that my lil bro is here, let me break it down. Yesterday at the picnic we recruited 10 brothers from like 10 different sets to make our muscle strong to take over No Love City. Bj is in charge of the muscle and as y'all know Tear Drop calls the shots for them and he also cops his work from me every other Friday. Today is Monday, so we got 4 days to have everybody ready and in place so we can hit all of his major spots while he's in my custody making a buy. While everybody's doing their part, I'm going to take him out. Then No Love City is ours, but once we take over I promise everyone who donated their mens 3 blocks, but they gone have to cop from me."

The old man spoke up first, "That sounds like a good plan, but don't you think you're moving on a lil too fast' cuz don't get it twisted, Tear Drop is a powerful man and cold blooded too. I think you're making it sound a lil too easy and moving too fast without doing more research."

"No disrespect, but I did my research for a month now and Friday, it's going down," Nuke relied.

"Don't get it wrong man, cause I'm riding with you all the way. I'm just making sure you know what we're up against."

Nuke tossed Bj a burn out phone and told him to call his soldiers and have them to meet up at the Mason Hall on 54th and Ashland, while he shoot to Indiana to get up with his country buddy Matt, who got any gun you want for dirt cheap. When he made it past the toll road he hit Matt on the phone.

Matt picked up on the second ring, "What's up my brother from a distant mother?" He knew not to say names over the phone.

Nuke let him know that he was only 15 minutes away.

Matt replied, "Ok, I'll see you when you get here."

Really Nuke was only 2 minutes away, but his lack of trust prevents him from giving anyone the chance to set him up.

Nuke pulled up in the back of the mechanic shop and blew his horn twice. The garage came open and he pulled in. Matt greeted him with, "That was a fast 15 minutes."

"Now you should know me by now, as much business as we do."

"What can a white boy do for you?" Matt asked.

Nuke pointed to the office because he refused to talk out in the open. Matt entered the office and went straight to his mini bar in the corner. "You want a drink," he offered to Nuke.

"Naw, I don't drink while I'm doing business."

"I got some Remy over here. I know how y'all like dark liquor," Matt invited.

Nuke was tempted, but decided to stay in control. "Let's just get down to business. Nuke then tossed a knot full of money on the desk. "I need all automatic machine guns and about 20 grenades. That's $10,000 and I got ten more when I get my delivery."

"Whoa, brother, you trying to start a war or something?"

"Come on buddy, I would never disrespect you like that."

"It's cool, just tell me how long it will take to get them."

"Give me a week."

"No disrespect, but I need them in 2 days, even if I have to come get them myself."

"Well, call me at 10 in the morning and I will give you an address and you just flip the numbers and come get them. I know you don't like talking on the phone and just bring me five, not ten. I owe you."

Bj and his team gathered in the Mason Hall with a map of all the main spots to hit. Everyone listened while he gave the orders. "I need every team to be on point and do their job. This is out meet up point when you finish and make sure you're not being followed. Oh, and one more thing, I got a cell phone for each team leader. It is only…and I mean only about business and not personal use. We have 3 days until show down. Keep a low profile and lay low till Friday. You're all dismissed. Hold up, one more thing, meet up here Thursday morning. I will have all the artillery for everyone. Keep yours at home!"

The next morning, Nuke and Bj drove out to Indiana, with a minivan following them. Tonya was driving the minivan. She runs a click of females that "comes in all shapes and forms of trouble from robbery to carjacking to murder and anything else that a hood n*gga could get into. Fifty percent of the n*ggas around fear her and her crew. The only reason she's on this trip herself and not sending someone else is because Nuke begged her to do it herself to alleviate the risk of something going wrong.

When they arrived at the pickup spot, everyone stayed in their cars while Nuke went in. He was leery because Matt wasn't there, but he made a phone call and was told who to see. He chirps Tonya on her Nextel and tells her to pull around the back. The loading process went as planned and the team on on their way back.

Nuke and Bj trailed Tonya back to Chicago. Thirty minutes into the ride, Nuke spotted the state troopers about 7 cars back. He chirped Tonya to inform her, as the trooper is now only 2 cars back. The trooper pulls in behind Nuke and starts running the license plates. Nuke holds his chirp in his lap as he gives Tonya orders in case he gets picked up or the try to get behind her.

The trooper stayed behind Nuke for about 2 or 3 miles before he merged into the passing lane. When he got a little bit in front of Nuke, he put his signal on as if he wanted to get in between Nuke and Tonya. Nuke was not letting that happen, so he pulled up as close aa he can get to Tonya' back bumper to block the license plates from the trooper.

The trooper then pulled up on the side of Tonya and signaled for her to pull over. At first she wasn't going to, but Nuke chirp her and told her to pull over. He had a plan. She pulled over and Nuke pulled over right in front of her so that the state trooper can get behind her. Once the state trooper put his car in park and was getting out of the car, Nuke yelled in the chirp to pull off.

Tonya did as she was told and by the time the trooper make it to his car, she had a nice lead on him. As the trooped tried to get in route, Nuke pulled off in front of him to slow him down. The trooper hit his sirens for Nuke to get out of the way, but Nuke didn't at this point. The trooper realized that they're together and that the minivan gots to be the main target. He tries to maneuver his way around Nuke to catch up with the van that's now almost out of his sight.

Nuke sees him in the rearview mirror on his walkie—talkie and he chirps to Tonya to tell her to get off at the next exit and take the streets. When the trooper got close on his tail Nuke tapped the brakes and the trooper rammed into him from the back and swerve out of control to the side of the road. Nuke kept on goin but knew not to get off the express way to prevent Tonya from getting caught.

Ten miles down the road, 3 state troopers pulled up behind him. One moved up on the right side, while one stayed behind and the other one took the left side to box him in. He put his right signal on to let them know he's surrendering. He don't care about the charge , as long as Tonya gets away. Before he even comes to a complete stop, he calls his broyer to let him know what's going on and to meet him at 11th police station.

The troopers approach his car with guns drawn, as if he committed a murder or something. "Put your hands where I can see them," one of the troopers orders.

Nuke and Bj both did as they were told.

One officer took the Nuke, while the others stood back ready to shoot. "Driver, take your right hand and stick it out the window and open the door from the outside, but keep your left hand up where I can see it."

Nuke did as he was told and put his hand on top of his head once he was out of the car. One of the officers handcuffed him, while the other ones focused on Bj. Once the officers had both men cuffed, they searched the car as if they knew for sure that something was in there.

After thirty minutes of searching pulling seats apart, and not finding anything, the officers decided to let them go until a call came over the radio about a van. Nuke looked stunned and shocked of thinking that Tonya was caught. It turned out to be another van. She was safe. One officer walked up and said that the sergeant said to charge them with attempt on a police officer and fleeing the crime scene.

At the police station, Nuke was in one room while Bj was being interrogated in another room. "So, Mr. Johnson, what were y'all doing coming from Indiana?" the officer glared.

"Sir, can you please call my broyer. I ain't saying anything till my broyer gets here," Bj responded.

"Oh, you are one of them smart asses who thinks your broyer's going to save you, but you have an attempt on a officer. You're going to need 2 broyers for this one, unless you want to give up your partner," the officer snapped back.

In the other room, Nuke was being told the same thing, as if that's all the officers' practice. After an hour of trying to get them to confess, their broyer shows up and orders for them to be released,, if they're not being charged. Bj is freed, while charges were pressed on Nuke, since he was the driver. The broyer told Bj that he would be at bond court in the morning and to bring a check for like $10,000 in case he got a low bond.

When Bj left the police station his first priority was to contact Tonya and make sure she made it safe and get the guns somewhere safe. He used his brother's cell phone to call her, because she is Nuke's connect and this was the first time Bj had met her.

"Hello, Nuke, everything alright on your end?" was the greeting.

"Aye, Tonya, this is Bj. I'm calling you from his phone cause he's at the 11th police station for attempt on a police officer and fleeing the scene."

"What the f*ck? How did that happen?" she shoots back.

"Tonya, tell me your location and I'm on my way to take you out to lunch cause I don't talk over phones."

"I'm on 65th and Mozart. Call me when you get on the block."

"OK, I'm like 15 minutes away."

Bj picked Tonya up and headed to a pizzeria on 63rd and

Richmond. It's owned by Mexicans, so it's a good spot to talk at without being eaves dropped on.

"So where did the attempt come in at?"

"Well, once you made it far up ahead of us, we knew it was hard for us to try and get away, so while the officer was riding our bumper trying to get around us, to catch up with you, Nuke tapped his brakes and the officer slammed into us and then spun around in the opposite direction."

"So how did y'all get caught?"

"We knew more state troopers will be after us if we stayed on the express, so you can make it safe on the streets."

"Let him know I said thanks for the sacrifice."

"It's cool. One hand washed the other."

"Tell him that the money he promised me' to give it to me in white…"

"I got you. I'll have it ready for you in a couple of hours when I send for that pack."

"Alright."

Bj dropped Tonya back off where he got her from. Before she got out of the car, she told him, "Since you got my number, you can use it for personal use too."

"I'll keep that in mind. Aye, Tonya, one more thing, I need you to go down to the court house and bond Nuke out."

"No problem, sexy, I'll have one of my down chicks with good paper work to take care of that, so it can be official."

"Here Tonya, take my number and call me when you want to cause I'm not a phone person."

Bj and Tonya exchanged numbers and went their separate ways. While driving back to the hood, Bj decided to call Sheena, since he hadn't talked to her all that day.

"Hello beautiful!" he said as she answered on the second ring. "You must have been waiting for me to call."

"Why you say that?"

"Well you answered the phone so quick."

"I had it in my hand, twirling it around and it started ringing."

"So you was waiting on me to call..."

"Actually, I was thinking about calling you but figured you were into something or handling some business. "

"Well, I was wondering if you wanted to stop by and watch a movie before it gets too late."

"That will be nice, but you have to have me back home before 1 a.m."

"No problem. I'll call you around 6 o'clock."

"Alright, Bryant, be careful."

"I will."

His next call was to inform Tiff about Nuke. This should have been his first call, but he didn't want to stress her out.

"Hello Tiff."

"And who is this?"

"This is Bryant."

"Oh, how are you doing, Bryant?"

"Fine, but I am calling to let you know that Nuke is locked up but he will be out tomorrow."

"What happened? Is he in some bad trouble? Where did he

63

get locked up at? And how did it happen?" Tiff asked about 10 questions before Bj could answer one.

"Tiff just be cool. He will explain it all when he gets out tomorrow. I just didn't want you to be thinking he stayed out all night."

"Thank you so much Bryant. Are you coming in tonight?"

"Yes, I'm coming home tonight. Do you need anything?"

"Just some orange juice and bread."

"Alright, I'll bring it in when I come."

"Be careful, Bryant."

"I will sis. Bye bye."

Tonya had the guns delivered to the Mason Hall as she was told. After Sal and Zeek finished packing them in safely, they were escorted on their way. Tonya and Bj sat in the hall talking about putting another crew together to help lure the other big bosses who weren't on the target yet. "Tonya, you just work on putting the girls together and I'll take care of everything else."

"I got you and can a sister get a taste of what you're working with under your pants?"

"Sur, but now ain't the time. Just give me a few days and I'll knock your back in."

Tonya purred like a cat, "Purr! I can't wait!"

"Oh, and here's the cash. I owe you and the check for Nuke's bond tomorrow. I'll give you a call tomorrow."

"You better," Tonya said in her seductive way before leaving.

On the way to get Sheena, Bj had Tonya on his mind, he was so close on taking her up on her offer right in the Mason Hall, but didn't want to mix business with pleasure in the same day.

Bj picked Sheena up and was heading home. They stopped at a store to get some snacks and the bread and orange juice that Tiff wanted. While Sheena was in the store her cell phone stared ringing. She looked at the caller ID and wondered why Bj was calling.

"What's wrong Bryant?"

"Nothing boo, I just want you to grab me a pack of Newport 100's and remember that I don't drink pop."

"I remember that but when did you start smoking cigarettes?"

"I've been smoking them. I just don't chain smoke like the average smoker."

"them things stank."

"Well, grab me some gum too mama."

Bj hung up the phone before she can say anything smart, but he knows she's going to have a lot to say when she gets back in the car.

When Sheena got in the car she had the cigarettes in her hand. She threw them in his lap. "Here smart ass. I'm trying to help you keep your lungs before you be needing mines. Keep smoking and you might see!"

Bj pulled off and turned the radio up so the argument wouldn't go any further.

Sheena and Bj set in the playroom watching "Jason's" lyrics. Bj tried to make a move on Sheena, but she told him she had a visitor. She tried to give him some head instead, but he oBjected to it because he couldn't make her feel good in return. When he told her why he didn't want it, she looked at him in a totally different way and her feelings grew stronger instantly. She knew she was in love!

After he dropped her off at her house he thought about turning Tonya's dream true sooner than planned, but then thought about the morning event and headed to his mother's house, but not before letting Tiff know he won't be back in.

Bj woke up with an urge to piss like a racehorse. While heading to the bathroom still half asleep, he didn't see his mother sitting in her rocking chair in the dining room. When he came out of the washroom he finally noticed her appearance and knew something was wrong.

"What's wrong ma?"

"Tiffany called me this morning about your brother getting locked up and that you was with him when it happened.."

Bj started wondering how she knew he was with him, but didn't want to ask her. "Ma, it was just a mistaking identity and since they wasn't able to catch who they was after, they harassed us instead."

"Bryant, I was born in the day time, but not yesterday."

"Your brother told Tiffany everything and she told me. All I want to tell you is, if trouble come at this door or the police knock on this door about you being in trouble, you're on your own."

"Ma, I'm not."

"Bryant, save it! You heard what I said."

"Yes, mama."

Bj got dressed and left the house. On his way to the Mason Hall, he called all of the captains of each team and told them to bring one person with them. "Ring...ring.." was the sound of his phone. He looked at the caller ID and didn't recognize the number, so he didn't answer it. Two minutes later, it started ringing again and from the same number.

He answered it, but didn't say anything until after the caller spoke. "Hello,, hello," the caller said.

"Who is this?" Bj said in an irritated tone.

"This is White Boy. You don't remember my voice N*gga? What the f*ck's up? When did you get home?"

"Last week, but I've been laying low, but now it's time to eat. White Boy, where you at right now?"

"I'm in Moe Town on 52nd and Green."

"Stay right there. I'll be there in 2 minutes to pick you up."

"I'll be sitting on the porch in the middle of the block."

"Alright, one."

Bj and White Boy had been friends since grade school. One day at school, White Boy was fighting this one kid in the back of Henderson School playground and he was doing a number on the kid even though the boy was taller than him and outweighed him by at least 10 pounds. Just when the kid couldn't take any more of the beat down, another kid jumps in and started beating he breaks off White Boy. I think if White Boy wasn't so tired he could have did the same damage to this kid, but Bj didn't like bullies and sneaky ones at that so he jumped in and showed his own skills and ever since then, if you saw Bj, you saw White

Boy.

Bj hit the unlock button and White Boy hopped in. White Boy looks at the car and asks, "Is this your ride, Bj?"

"Yeah, this me. You like it?"

"Hell, yeah, this b*tch raw as f*ck!"

"Give me a couple of weeks and you'll be sitting on something nice."

"That's what I'm talking about. Bj, where you getting money at?"

"That's why I came to pick you up. Me and my brother putting something together and I want you to be my right hand man."

"You know I got your back a 100%. Just tell me what I need to do."

Bj Explained his plan to White Boy on the way back to the Mason Hall. The other guys were waiting for them when they arrived. Everyone got quiet when Bj and White Boy walked into the hall.

Bj begins, "Fellas, I like for y'all to meet my right hand man, White Boy. I've told him about our plan for this Friday. I would expect for you all to treat him with the same respect as you give me. I'm putting him in charge of half of this operation. You, you, you and you, y'all teams are called Team Red and I'm in control of y'all. The other half of y'all is called Team Rum. When ever a job is complete and everyone is together our code is "RedRum". So on Friday when everyone is in place and waiting for the word, when you hear "RedRum" everything starts. Does anyone have something to say?"

One man shouts, "Let's get it on!"

Nuke was released on a $10,000 bond and was on his way to meet Bj and White Boy to discuss the last plan to the puzzle.

Friday came quick and Nuke couldn't wait. "Hello, bro-bro, what's happening ?"

"Same old, same oh, you good?"

"Yeah, I'm good."

"Well, I'll see you at the same time as always."

"OK, holla."

Aye, lil bro, I just got off the phone with homie. He was referring to Tear Drop. 'And everything's a go for today. We supposed to meet up at five this evening, so have your mens ready at 4 and when your phone ring and my number show up, give your man's the go ahead.'"

"That's what I'm talking about."

"Team Red, are you in position?"

"That's a green light!"

Team Rum are you in position?"

"That's a green light!"

"OK. wait for the final word…"

Nuke sat waiting for Tear Drop to show up in the back of the warehouse, while his team held their position. He has 2 men hiding behind the dumpster, which is about 5 feet from where he parked and four more in the Impala by the last entrance.

Tear Drop's men pulled up and gave Nuke a nod as they kept riding to park next to the Impala. Nuke and Tear Drop never get their hands dirty. That's where the mens in the cars come in

69

at. Nuke's guys hold the drugs while Tear Drop's guys hold the money.

Tear Drop rides up on the side of Nuke and hit the horn for Nuke to come get in the car with him. Nuke hesitated for a second cause any time they did business Tear Drop came and got in his car.

Nuke thought to himself that something's not right, but didn't let it stop him cause of the plan and the home field advantage he has, so he exited his car and got in with Tear Drop. He did dial Bj and let it ring twice before hanging up. Bj hits the chirp button and yelled "RedRum' to let them know the time is NOW!

"How's everything going for bro-bro?" Tear Drop asked as Nuke got in the car. "What's with the change of plan?" Nuke asked.

"Oh, it's nothing. I just sprung my ankle yesterday playing ball. That's why I signaled you to join me."

"You need to leave that court to them youngins before you catch a heart attack out there."

"I still got it in me to be 38 years old. bro-bro, I want to let you know that the next time we meet my order goinna be double cause I got these out of towners who wants to spend some money."

"That's cool, you let me know in advance."

"Well, besides that everything's cool on your end?"

"Yeah, I'm gravy."

Tear Drop flicked the lights to let his men know that now is the time to do the transaction. When Tear Drop's men passed the duffle bag to the driver, Nuke upped his Glock 45 and told Tear Drop not to move. Tear Drop looked ahead as Nuke's guys opened fire on his men.

"This what you on bro-bro?"

"Yeah, this is what I'm on. This hood aint' big enough for both of us and I want your land."

"You can have that sh*t just let me go." Tear Drop didn't see the 3 guys coming along the side of his car.. As soon as Nuke stepped out of the car, Tear Drop put the car in drive and tried to pull off as a flurry of bullets hit him in the back of his neck and all over his back.

Tear Drop slammed into the pole. Nuke never did see the Buick that was parked 10 cars behind him and Tear Drop until he heard tires screeching in his direction sending a substantial amount of bullets his way. He ducked behind his car and got in on the passenger side.

All 4 of Nuke's men that were in the Impala started shooting at the Buick, as those men tried to put Tear Drop into their car. Their passenger was hit twice in the chest as he tried to get back in. The Buick made a u-turn and fled the scene, but not without getting more bullet hole in their car from the 2 men that was hiding behind the dumpster.

Nuke scooted over the driver's seat and pulled alongside of Tear Drop's car, remembering that he touched the passenger door to get in. He hopped out but almost fell as he now realizes that he has been shot in the right leg. He hopped over and wiped the handle clean, then hopped back to his car. He motioned for the 2 guys to get in as he heard the sirens from a distance away.

Nuke pulled off before the guy in the back seat can get fully in.

On the other side of town, team RedRum done ran in 8 different spots and came out with close to $10,000 in drugs and over $25,000 in cash. Two guys from Team Red was murdered and one from Team Rum.

Bj and White Boy were waiting for Nuke to return. Bj yelled to his guys, "Hold that noise for a second."

"Hello, where you at big bro?" Bj asked Nuke.

"I'm on my way to Aunt Dorothy's house to get my wound cleaned. I've been shot in the lag and I can't go to the hospital cause they going to be asking all types of questions," Nuke answered.

"I'm gone meet you there in 20 minutes."

"Everything alright on your end?"

"I'll holla at you when I get to you."

"Aye, White Boy, I need to go meet my bro right quick, so I need you to hold this down tilll I get back. In fact, just split all the drugs and money amongst the team and stash all the weapons on the 3rd floor and meet me at my Aunt Dorothy's house."

"I don't have no ride, Bj"

"Here, take my keys. I'm goin walk around the corner to Kisha's house and have her to drop me off."

"Here J take this 380. It's clean."

"I'm cool. I got this baby Glock on me."

"Be safe Bj and watch your back."

"I'ma hit your horn as soon as I leave from here."

"Alright one."

Bj and White Boy embrace each other and then walk

separate ways.

As Bj reached the front door of his aunt's house, all he could hear is his big brother yelling. "It's burning, Auntie! Ah, sh*t!"

"You better watch your damn mouth in here. Is you crazy or something? You lucky it went in and out without damaging nothing."

"Here take these extra strength Tylenols and stop whining like a lil girl."

"This sh.., I mean stuff hurts."

"You better be glad you caught that word cause I was gonna punch you in that leg and have you really hollering like a pig under a gate."

"Please don't do that Tee-Tee! Aye li bro you got some weed on you?"

"No, but White Boy on his way. I can call him and tell him to   stop   and   get   some."
"Yeah, call him."

"I don't care what y'all do, but you're not smoking that stuff in here."

"Mama always said its better to smoke at home than outside."

"I ain't yo' mama and speaking of my sister, let me call her and let her know what happened."

"Tee-Tee, please don't call her. That woman will have a heart attack. She already stressing for nothing, cause I just bonded out of jail. Lord knows this will take her bout over the edge."

"Alright, I'ma keep my mouth closed this time,, but you

better come here every day for a week, so I can clean that wound before it get infected."

"Aye, White Boy, where you at?"

"I'm 2 blocks away. Why? What's up?"

"I was going to tell you to stop and get some smokes." "I got a blunt and a half, but if you wants some more, I'll turn around."

"Naw, that's cool for right now."

"Alright, I'm pulling up right now. Come one out."

"Just park and come in."

"Man your aunt gonna let us blast the crib out?"

"No, we gone chill on the back porch."

White Boy walked into the house with his hat smack to the left. "How are you doing Auntie Dorothy?"

"I'm fine but gonna be feeling like Leila Ali, if you don't take that hat off in my house."

"I'm sorry Tee-Tee."

"What's up White Boy?"

"What's up Nuke?"

"When you get out White Boy?"

"Oh, I been home for a few weeks now. Just trying to stary out of them people's way."

"That's what's up!"

"Aki, how's your mother doing?"

"She's fine, just always stuck at that shop."

"Tell her that I'm coming down there next week to get my hair done."

"Here's her cell phone number. Call her."

"Hold on, let me get my phone book."

"Aye, White Boy, we gonna be on the back porch rolling up. Come one lil bro, help me back there."

The three smoked and talked for hours until Nuke got a call about Tear Drop's condition. The word on the streets is that he's in a coma and has a good chance of pulling through. Tonya says she has a girl that works on the same floor he's on and will keep her updated on his condition.

The news states that they have no leads and is offering $5,000 on the killers or any information that can lead them in the right direction.

Bj woke up the next morning, with business on his mind. He called a meeting with his team to meet up at headquarters in one hour. When everyone arrived, Bj went right into boss mode.

"Jake, you in charge fo Terror Town and y'all can set up shop from 56 to 59th and Loomis. Tommy Gun from Ducktown, you got the same amount of blocks, but you're on Throop. Shawn Shawn, form Crank Town, you got May Street. Mike Mike from Foster Park, you Carpenter and Tye Murder from Rocket City and Boo Man from Stone Tez, y'all gone team up and be the hitters."

"Hello, Nuke,"

"Yeah what's going on, Tonya?

"Is there somewhere I can meet you right now?"

""Can it wait till later on?"

"No! this is important!"

""Alright, I'll see you in 20 minutes."

"Alright.."

Nuke's visit with Tonya was not what he waned to hear. Tear Drop ws shipped to an undercover hospital for security reasons for his health and other disclosed information.

Bj answered the phone on the first ring. Nuke said, "Aye, lil bro, we need to meet ASAP."

"Ok, I'll see you soon."

Nuke waited out front as Bj pulled up in front of their Auntie Dorothy's house. "Let's go around the block and sit on the porch," Nuke says as they pulled away.

"Lil bro, I just came from seeing Tonya and her source at the hospital said that he was moved to a confidential hospital for security reasons and disclosed information. I don't know if he's tricking but we have to make sure that our end is air tight. I think we should close down some of them new spots that we took."

"Big bro, it's only been a week and the money is rolling in real good and plus, we promise them spots for their help. We can't just take it from them."

"Aye, lil bro, I feel you but we have to come up with something to make sure we're secure cause what good is the money when we can't spend it?"

"You're right big bro. Let's just give it a few days and see what we can come up with."

"Alright, just stay off the streets for a few days till we hear something else about home boy."

Bj and Sheena was having a good time till he received a call saying that Shawn from Crank Town was getting raided and that 3 of his guys were arrested for guns and drugs.

"Sheena, you want to stay at my house or go home cause

there's some important stuff that just came up and it has to be taken care of."

"Baby, please don't go. I been having a bad feeling for a few days now and right no, my stomach is really turning."

"Bay, I'll be back in a hour. I promise everything's goin be alright."

Bay, please just stay. Can you call Nuke and have him to do it?"

"Bay, just chill. It's only gone be a quick run, right quick."

"I have a feeling that something about to happen…"

"Bay don't talk like that."

"Bryant, there's something I want to tell you."

"Sheena, it got to wait till I get back," he said as he closed the door behind him before she got another word out.

Bj called a broyer to meet his boys at the police station and called Nuke to let him know to meet him at their gossip place. As soon as he hung up the phone, he had a text message from Sheena saying, "I was trying to tell you that I'm pregnant and that I'm ready to move in with you." Bj didn't know what to say to the news he had just received due to all the stuff that's been going on lately. He texted her back, "I love you and see you soon," with smiley faces after the words.

As he gets to his auntie's block, he sees police lights in the middle of the block, so he backs up and parks on the side street and walks down the block to see what's wrong. As he gets closer, he sees his brother's car in the middle of the street with another police car in the front of him, so he can't go anywhere.

77

Dorothy was making a big scene, so he knew something wasn't wrong. He took the hint and turned around and headed back to his car.

At the police station, Nuke was getting finger printed for possession of an unregistered firearm. The Turn Key yelled out, "Mr. Barker, do you want to make a collect call?"

"Yes!"

"Well, step over there. You have 5 minutes to make your call."

The first person Nuke called was Bj to have him get down there and bond him out before they put a bond hold on him. Then he called his wife, Tiffany, to let her know what's going on.

Bj made it to the police station to bond his brother out but was told he would have to wait until bond court in the morning at the county jail.

While laying in the cold cell at the police station, Nuke's mind was roaming in a hundred different directions, until he heard his name being called. "Mr. Barker, there's someone here to talk to you."

First he thought it was his broyer, but thought why would he be here if I've already been charged?

A white man in a suit looking like Shawn O'Connor and a heavy set black man looking like Forest Whitaker was standing in front of the cell.

"My name is Officer Brady and this is my partner, Officer brown and we're from Area 1 headquarters homicide unit. We would like to ask you a few questions."

"Well, the number is 555-1500 and his name is Frank. He is

my broyer. Call him and when he gets here come back and get me," was Nuke's reply.

Nuke laid back down as the detectives left thinking to himself, "How in the hell, I'm a suspect? unless this bitch ass n*gga Tear Drop is tricking. I got to hurry up and get out of here as soon as I get a bond."

White Boy was standing on the corner when this fine ass girl looking like a black version of Jessica Alba, pulled up in a red Maxima, asking for Bj. He was so blinded by her beauty that he didn't see the black bronco pulling up with the passenger side window down exposing a masked man holding what could be mistaken as a robo cop gun from a distance because of the size.

Boom, boom, boom was al you heard from the gun as the assassin aimed to kill. White Boy was hit in the shoulder and grazed in the neck as he was knocked off his feet. The female in the Maxima pulled off as soon as she heard the first shot, but not without getting a hole in the side of her car.

Scrap and Pooka rushed over to White Boy's side as he was going in and out of consciousness due to the rapid loss of blood.

"Help me get him in the car Pooka. We can't wait for the ambulance. He's losing a lot of blood," Scrap said.

Once in the car, Pooka applied pressure to the wound to slow the bleeding while Scrap ran every light trying to get to the hospital. "Hold on White Boy. Stay with me. We're almost there, just stay with me bro."

"Bj, this is Scrap. White Boy just got hit up and we got him in the back seat on our way to the hospital."

"No, take him to my Auntie's house," Bj shot back.

79

"We can't, bro, he's in bad shape."

"Alright, stay there. I'm on my way."

White Boy was rushed into surgery at St. Menard hospital. The nurse wouldn't let anyone see him while he was in critical condition because his vital signs were stilll low due to the amount of blood lost. The detective was waiting patiently to get their chance to questions White Boy and try to bring the shooting to a halt.

Bj made it to the hospital in no time. As soon as he got off the elevator, Pooka and Scrap rushed towards him with blood all over their clothes.

"What happened bro," was Bj's immediate question.

"Let's step outside and talk these pigs been up here all day sweating the hallway, like they in a marathon to beat us in there to talk to White Boy."

Outside Bj paced back and forward smoking on a Newport, while Scrap explained what happened to White Boy.

"Who y'all think could have tried to take him out?"

"I don't know bro, but he was standing up to a red Maxima when it went down. I couldn't see the chick, but she looked brown skinned."

"A red Maxima? Did it have a sunroof?"

"I think so."

"What kind of car was the shooter in?"

"A black bronco, but the passenger had on a mask."

"Yeah, check this out, y'all go get a change of clothes and hit my phone when it get dark. I think I know who was in that Maxima."

Nuke was sitting the in the interrogation room with his broyer waiting for the 2 detectives to come in and start their questioning. The black detective who came to his cell yesterday was the first to enter the room, followed by his partner.

Nuke's broyer stood up and introduced himself with his business card in his hand. "My name is Frank. I'm here to represent Mr. Barker. Is my client under arrest or a suspect in any type of crime?"

"We just want to ask him a few questions. It would help us get some type of lead in the investigation."

The detectives pressed play on the recorder and stated his questioning. "Today is June 3rd and it is 6:42 pm and I, Detective brown and my partner, Detective Brady, from Area 1 headquarters homicide unit are here with Mr. Barker and his attorney, Mr. Frank for questioning."

"Mr. Barker, where were you last Friday between 5 and 6 o'clock?"

Nuke was about to answer until Frank tapped him on the hand. "If my client is not being charged then there's no need for an alibi."

"Well, Mr. Frank, four men were killed and one in the coma and our client's finger prints were on the inside of the victim's car, who's in the coma and we're trying to get as much information as we can."

"Well, detectives, if my client is not being charged for anything, I'd like for him to be taken back to his cell and if you have any more questions for him, to avoid a bro suit please call me first."

The detectives gave Mr. Frank a look as it he was a criminal, as he stood up and walked out of the interrogation room, with his client, feeling as if he's just beat a trial, but also knowing this is not the end.

Bj left the hospital in a blurry state of mind because of all the things that's been happening this past week, especially not knowing where the hits were coming from. As he drove in silence contemplating his next move, his phone started vibrating. He looked at the caller ID and sees Tonya's number.

"Hello, what's up Bj?" she asked.

"Sh*t, I wish I knew."

"I heard about what happened to White Boy. Is he alright?"

"Yeah, he cool. He just lost a lot of blood, so they got him hooked up to all them damn machines, but Tonya, what's up? have you heard anything or know anything about a black 2 door bronco?"

"A 2 door bronco? Uh, let me see. I remember seeing a black bronco, but I can't put my finger on it. When it comes to me, best believe you will be the first to know."

As Bj talked on the phone, he kept his eyes on the rearview mirror cause it seems like this same Ford Taurus been following him ever since he left the hospital. "Aye Tonya, where you at right now?"

"I just came from one of my customer's spot. Why?"

"Is you holding boo?"

"Never leave home without it. Why, do you need it?"

"This Ford Taurus been following me since I left the hospital."

"What color is ti?"

"Navy blue."

"Do it have tinted windows?"

"Yeah, that's what made me keep an eye on it."

"Aye, B.J, them dudes ride with dude them. I'm right here on 63rd and Racine."

"Where you at?"

"I'm on 59hth and Ashland, heading towards 55th."

"B.J, I'm gone meet you on 55th and Racine. I'm gone get behind them and light up the night like the 4th of July. I'm in a gray Malibu, so when you see me turn and get on the other side of Garfield."

"OK, see you there."

Bj drove as if everything was cool, but something told him that this wasn't going to play out right. It was just a gut feeling that can go either way.

When he reached Elizabeth, which is one block from Racine, the Ford Taurus got exactly behind him and now he could see that it was 2 men in the front seat and maybe one more in the back seat.

When he reached Racine, the light had just turned green and Tonya sat facing him at the light, which put him at ease. So he made the left turn. Tonya then ran the red light to get behind the Taurus, instead of the Taurus getting behind Bj. They pulled along side of him, but when Bj noticed the back window down he tried to pull off but the traffic was coming too quick.

The person in the back seat opened fire on Bj's car with a Mac Ten. The bullets were coming so fast that Bj couldn't lift up

83

to see if the coast was clear for him to try to get away, but sitting in one spot was like asking to die or should I say, waiting to die.

Tonya pulled on the side of the Taurus and started firing her Eagle all up in the back seat. This brought the shots from the Mac Ten to a halt. The driver wantd to pull off as well, but the traffic was still coming. He decided to take his chances as he sideswiped the back of the last car that was trying to make the light.

Tonya jumped out of her car and ran up to Bj's to make sure he's alright, but all she could see was him slumped over in the seat with his chest moving up and down as if he's trying to catch his breath.

"Bj, hold on, baby, don't die on me, please baby, don't die on me. Just hold on," Tonya hopped out of the car and flagged down a car with 2 guys in it. The guys didn't want to stop at first because she was holding a gun in her hand. But when the driver saw the car that was in the middle with bullet holes in it, he pulled over and hopped out.

Tonya reached out to him with 5 one hundred dollar bills in her hand, "here take this money. All I need is for you to have your friend drive my car to the hospital and I can take it from there."

Before the guy can answer her she was already in the driver's seat of Bj's car pulling off. Both guys pulled off behind her heading towards the hospital.

The nurse came out to talk to Tonya about his condition, "Miss, can I talk to you for a second?"

"Yes, ma'm. Is he alright?"

"Yes, he's alright. It's a good thing that the bullet went in and out cause if not it would have damaged his abdomen."

"When can I see him?"

"The nurse is in there wrapping his bandage and as soon as she's finished, he can be discharged."

"Really?"

"Yes, it was just a flesh wound. HE just had a panic attack."

Tonya and Bj left the hospital before the police can get there to question them. Tonya had 2 cars full of females waiting outside with a spare car for her and Bj to ride home alone in.

"Aye, Tonya thanks a lot for having my back today. I probably would be dead if it wasn't for you."

"Don't say that boo. You're a soldier, cause if you wasn't I wouldn't even f*ck with you, and plus I like your style."

"Yeah, Shorty, that's real. Remember what we talked about with putting the female click together?"

"Yeah, I don't forget nothing, not even when you promised to break my back in but now I see you're sore, so we gone have to put that on hold."

"For real, Tonya, we need to put them girls together."

"Boy, I already got them together. I'm just waiting on you."

Nuke was going through the process at the county jail, when he ran into Shawn Shawn's guys that were caught in the raid. "What's up with y'all? What the f*ck happened?"

"Aye, I think somebody's dropping a dime on us for them to run in the way they did."

"What do you mean?"

"Cause they came right in and went straight to both of the

85

stash spots."

"Yeah, who all be in the spot with y'all?"

"Me, Craig, Wheatie and Wayne Wayne, and they let Wayne Wanye go."

"Well, there you go. Ain't no need to say no more."

"How much is y'all bond?"

"$12,500. to walk."

"Yeah, Aye, look y'all at the first court date ask for a bond reduction to at least $10,000 and if they don't we still gone come get y'all. It's just that they just gave me a $20,000 bond and plus I'm already out on a $10,000 bond, so it's tight but don't count me out."

"Aye, Nuke, did you hear about White Boy?"

"My people's say he's in the hospital. They say he got hit up pretty bad, but they didn't go into details over the phone."

"Yeah, I'm call my lil bro and see what happened. Y'all just do what I said and I got y'all."

Bj sat at Tonya's house waiting for the girls to arrive, so he can meet them. In the midst of waiting, Tonya got a lil touchy and started massaging his penis. He pushed her hand away cause he was stilll in pain and knew if he let her keep going he wouldn't be able to finish. She got a lil upset but didn't show it because of what the future might hold.

An hour later, Tonya woke Bj up out of his rest to let him know that the girls had arrived. Each girl was to come up one by one and give their name and resume, as if they were in some type of job interview.

The first girl that came up was named Mystery. She looked

86

like she was from Brazil with her fbroless skin and thick hips and an ass that would give Buffy a run for her money. Tonya told her to show her specialty and in one swift motion, 3 razonrs appeared on the top of her tongue and started moving in a slci rotation. Let's call this the "Kiss of Death".

Next up was Coco. She was as black as charcoal but had the whitest eyes. that Bj had ever seen. She had a nice body as well. Bj figured that 80 out of 100 men would come at her. Her specialty is her ability to pinpoint a person's pressure point which causes them to stop breathing instantly. The interviews lasted for over an hour, until Bj was happy with all the killing talent that came in front of him.

When Nuke made it up to his tier at the County jail, the first thing he did was run to the phone to call his wife. "You have a collect call from an inmate at the County jail, to accept press one or just say 'Yes'"

Tiff pressed one0 quickly. "Hello, bay, what's up?"

"They ain't came up here to bond me out yet!"

"Yeah, honey they been up there all morning. They should be calling you any minute now."

"Click over and call my lil brother on 3way."

"Alright hold on.

"Yo, big bro, what's up?"

"Sh*t that' what! I'm trying to find out. I know I shouldn't have made it on deck. Did they pay my bond or what??"

"Yeah, Frank called me and said that everything was taken care of. Just be cool. If you're not out tonight, I'm gone have Frank out there in the morning."

"Aye, lil bro, is White Boy alright?"

"He's cool, just a li f*cked up, but Shorty a survivor."

"Is you on top of that sh*t out there?"

"I got this big bro, just be cool till tomorrow, if they call you tonight, hit my horn and I'll be there to pick you up.

Bj left Tonya's house and was heading home until Sheena called him wondering why she hadn't heard from him since the text message. So, he changed course and headed over to her place.

On the way to Sheena's house, he decided to stop by his mother's house because he hadn't talked to her in almost a week and know he was working her nerves due to the lack of communication and plus like the saying goes, "Momma knows when her son is doing wrong when the scenery change from seeing to not seeing."

When Bj walked in his mother's house, which used to be his home, he could feel a vibe of loneliness, emptiness, forgotten and teariness, which stands for left, cause that's how he felt at this moment, as he thinks about him being out in th streets and not knowing how his mother is doing or feeling.

As he walks to the dining room, he can hear the TV playing in his mother's room, so he knows she' awake. "Stella, I'm home," he calls. No answer. He calls again, "Stella, is you in there?" as he made it to the room, which was empty, but it looks like she was just in there. He heads toward the kitchen still searching for her, until he hears the toilet flush and then the bathroom door opens. "Ma, how you doing?" Bj asks.

"What are you doing in my house?" Mama snaps.

"Ma, I came by to see how you is doing and plus I'm your son."

"Didn't I tell you twice that once you start the steets to forget about me and my house?"

"Ma, it's not like that."

"Yes, it is. What you think I'm stupid or something? No, I haven't seen or heard from you in weeks and you tell it ain't like that. I do respect the fact that you did leave and I didn't have to put you out."

"Ma, I love you dearly, but something's you just can't avoid and plus I put in all them applications and not one of them called me back. I can't depend on you and my brothers to take care of me all the time. I'm getting grown."

"Well, for you information, Mr. You had 2 job interviews this week, but you don't answer your phone. I've been calling you all week."

"Ma, I just want you not to give up on me because I'm doing wrong."

"Sweetie, I will always love you, but I will not condone in the negativity that you're in."

"That's all I ask, Ma. I just felt that we needed to have this conversation cause it was eating at me and I didn't know how to face you with it without hurting you."

"Bryant, I already knew what was going on, just cause I'm not out there in those no good street don't mean that I'm blind to what's going on."

"Ma, I love you."

"And I love you too honey."

"Well, I'm going to head over to Sheena's house."

"Ok, baby, be careful out there and whenever you get tired of them streets, my door is always open!"

"Okay, Ma, I'll call you tomorrow."

As Bj pulled on Sheena's block, he called her to let her know to come open the door. As he got out of the car, he looked around to make sure no one was following him. As he walks up the steps, he sees Sheena in he door way with what seems like panties and a bra. On second glance, it was boy shorts and a sports bra. He can feel his man rising as he stares at what looks like a camel's foot between her legs. "What's up Bay?"

"I don't know why you lusting at me like that baby boy. Ain't nothing happening tonight brother. You on punishment."

"What you talking about? I can't look?"

"Sure you can I just thought I would let you know ahead of time."

"Girl move out the way and let me in," as he walked passed her she pushed him in the lower back, not knowing that he' been shot. He jumped and winced at the same time from the pain in his side.

"What's wrong bay? Let me see!"

"I've been shot in the side this morning."

"What, why didn't you call me?"

"Cause it went in and out and I was trying to get out the hospital before the police came to ask questions."

"So, why didn't you call me when you left the hospital?"

"Bay, I'm not trying to argue tonight. I didn't want you to panic and start worrying. I just left my mother's house and she don't even know."

"Bryant, if I'm your girl, I'm supposed to know about sh*t like this as soon as it happens, not after everything's done. Where do we stand with our trust? Bryant, answer that!" she replied as the tears started falling like the Buckingham Fountain.

Bj reached to console her but she tried to pull away as she kept demanding for an answer.

"T, that's why I'm here, baby, cause you mean everything to me. This is the only place I want to be as I heal and you're the only person that I want to help me heal."

"Bryant, what happened? Who shot you and why someone want to kill you Bryant? Ain't you tired of the drama in your life, huh?"

"Calm down, you looking at things the wrong way. Let's just talk about all this in the morning. I mean everything, baby. I'm tired right now and my side is killing me."

"Do you need some pain pills?"

"Please, Bay. Do you got some?"

Sheena returned with some pain pills and a glass of orange juice.

Sheena and Bj laid in the bed in each other's arms enjoying each other's thoughts.

"T I want to ask you something," he said.

She turned around to face him.

"I, I know this might be kind of early but when the heart feels the way it feels then its never early..." as he reached for her hand and put a 3 carat diamond on her finger. "Will you marry me?"

91

"Yes, I will marry you.. Yes, I will!"

He kissed her on her forehead and wiped away the tears that were falling from her eyes. "Bay I know you're pregnant and I want you to have the baby, but if you're not ready cause of your schooling and you working, I can understand…"

"Bay, I was thinking the same thing and I didn't know how to come to you with it, so I'm glad that you understand."

"T whatever you with, I'm with you 100%. You're my heart, my soul, my everything and I will love you forever."

"Me, also baby!"

When Bj woke up the next morning, Sheena was already out of the bed and in the kitchen cooking and talking on the phone at the same time when he entered. He walked up behind her and kissed her on the neck and spoke, "Good morning."

She ended her conversation with "Girl, I'm gone to talk to you later. My finance is trying to make me stop cooking and lay his ass on the table and ride him like its no tomorrow, while he's kissing me on my neck. Girl bye, I'll talk to you later."

Bj and Sheena sat at the table eating and talking. He told her about everything that's been going on since he's been home. He also explains to her that in order to get away from it, they will have to leave the state, which was the best thing she heard throughout the conversation, but that wasn't an option for him. He makes people run out of state, not the other way around. He also told her about the female crew he's putting together and no – she didn't like that idea, but she is sticking by her man.

"Demarcus Barker, you have an attorney visit. Be ready in 10 minutes." Nuke was sitting at the table with 3 Latin Kings playing copy coo, a Mexican dominoes game. "Aye Flaco, I'm bout to go see what this broyer talking about. I'll be back, plus you lucky cause I was about to kick y'all ass."

"Yeah, whatever bro. We will wait for you to come back cause I want my lunch snack," Flaco replied.

Flaco was the one that was on the news. He had gotten caught transporting 2,000 keys of cocaine and 13 crates of AK 47 riffles. He has a $30 million dollar bond and says that he's going to bond out. He holds a building spot for the Latin Kings in Division 9.

The other 2 players, Julio, has a building spot for the Saints and the other one is a Latin Count, who calls the shots for all the Counts in the county jail.

Nuke came off his visit mad as hell cause he's not going to be able to bond out. The broyer told him it's going to take a few months to get the hold lifted cause he doesn't have a judge yet. So when he got back on his deck, he went straight to the phone to call his lil brother and his wife to let them know what's going on.

White Boy was finally coming back to his normal self. He's been in stable condition for 2 days now and every 30 minutes the detective is bum rushing his room hoping for some information, as to him almost losing his life, but like the soldier he is the detective keeps coming up empty.

Scrap called Bj to inform him that White Boy was allowed to have visits now and that him and Pooka was just walking in the door.

"Tell him that I'm on my way there," was Bj's quick reply.

93

"OK, Bj," Scrap said, but the line went dead.

While Bj was driving to the hospital, he happens to see a red Maxima drive past him in the opposite direction, but then he notices that it is an old lady driving. It was then it hit him who was driving the red Maxima when White Boy got shot.

Bj dialed a number and she picked up on the second ring. "Curlin' what's up?" she answers.

"My life, that's what's up and that I do want so I'm not f*cking with you!

"Hold on Shorty. What's all that for?"

"I've been calling your phone for 2 days now and you sending it straight to the voice mail. I guess you don't care how I'm doing or if I got shot."

"Huh?"

"Shorty, I was told that my mans was talking to a girl in a red Maxima when he got shot, but I couldn't put my finger on it."

"Is he OK?"

"Yeah, I'm on my way up there to see him right now."

"Curlin did you see who was in that truck?"

"No, but I know they saw my car, so I got my car painted and my license plates changed, cause I'm not dying for no one."

"Girl, you cool. Ain't no one trying to hurt you girl."

"Sh*t y'all out here crazy."

"Curlin can I see you later on. I'm bout to walk in this hospital?"

"Sure, call my phone and tell White Boy to get well."

"Alright Shorty."

94

Bj walked in the hospital room where Pooka and Scrap were sitting down talking to White Boy. "Aye,, li bro, what's up?"

"Sh*t trying to get out this b*tch and finish this war that we in," was White Boy's reply.

"Be cool man and heal. They gone get theirs, whoever they is."

"The nurse said I should be out in another week, you know."

"That's what's happening."

"Aye, B.J you cool," Pooka said.

"Yeah, why you say that?" Bj responded.

"We was trying to call you the other night when we changed out clothes and you wasn't answering your phone."

"I'm cool, just got into a lil something, something."

"We heard about some dudes trying to take you out, so we came up to the hospital and they said you checked out already."

White Boy sat there in a daze after just hearing that his man's life was almost taken right after his. Now he really wanted to check out. "Aye, B.J, I got to get out of here quick. Whoever these n*ggas is, they gone feel it big time!"

"Just be cool," White Boy," Bj assured him.

"What you mean? I'm laying in this bitch, almost lost my life and you talking about be cool? It's on!" White Boy shot back.

"White Boy, be cool my n*gga. I feel the same way you feel. They also tried to take my life too. Do you see me loosing my mind trying to go out there and do sh*t without thinking? We're thinkers, not dummies. All we know is some one is trying to take us out. It could be anybody. We don't know where that n*gga at or what hospital he's in. So, if he's sending the hits, then they watching everything waiting for us to strike," Bj explained.

"B.J, if it's him, then why the hell they up here trying to question me?"

"You're right. White Boy just be cool till you get out. I need you in full recovery when you come home. Nuke is locked up with no bond, so we have to run everything out here and I need you with a clear mind. I got a team of females that I put together and they out there working. When I leave here I'm going to meet up with Tonya. She should have some info for me."

"Be careful out there bro."

"I am bro-bro. Aye, Pooka and Scrap, tomorrow morning go get y'all some rental cars but not in y'all's names and meet me at the hall at 11 am." Bj instructed.

"Alright J."

"Aye, White Boy,"

"Yo?"

"Your man down there still working?"

"It's always working! I didn't get hit down there."

"Well, I got this bitch on her way up here to blow your brains back n*gga."

"Well, send her here then."

"Alright, I'ma holla at y'all later and call me if you need anything.

"I got you bro and be careful out there."

"Yo, Tonya, what's up baby?"

"You must was reading my mind," she replied. "Cause I was

just dialing your number."

"Yeah that sounds like some good news!"

"Boy, ain't you gone like this."

"Where at?"

"My place across Western Ave."

"Be therein thirty."

"If you can make it in twenty, I'll reward you."

"Don't call my bluff."

"We will see then."

Bj made it there in twenty minutes but she didn't care, as long as he made it. When Bj knocked on the door, Tonya yelled for him to come in. He twisted the knob and the door came open. He didn't know what to expect, but he knew she was on some feisty sh*t as the place looks all romantic with the music playing low and what looks like a candlelight dinner on the dining room table. "Tonya, where you at girl?" was his question.

:What? You're in a rush?" she said as she came out of the kitchen with an ice bucket, 2 glasses, a bottle of rose Moet.

"I see you on some hot sh*t."

"How you know I came over here for this?" Bj asked.

"Well, I figure if you made the time, then I can stick to my word as well." she said.

"You're not going to be satisfied till I knock your back in."

"Well, I was hoping that tonight be that night," as she dropped the robe she had been wearing.

Bj's only thought was, "Damn, does she have a body!"

She stood before him with a red and black see thru panty and bra set on with the leg lace to go with it and to top it off, she had on some pumps to match. Bj started taking his clothes of right in the dining room. "Girl, tonight is your lucky night!"

"Calm down boo, we got all night of fun."

"Sorry, baby, but I got a fiancé and ain't no staying out all night."

"What some body got lucky before I put my lick down?" she asked as she licked her tongue out which hung past her chin like she's got some snake in her blood.

"Yeah, she lucky, if that's what yo want to call it, but we can have bout 4 hours of fun."

"That's enough time for me or should I say too much time."

He walked toward her and grabbed her hips as Marvin Gaye sang in the background, "Let's get it on, ah baby, let's get it on."

Bj kissed her neck as he pulled her bra off exposing her firm C cup breasts. He kissed his way down to her left nipple and then to the right, as she moaned in pleasure. She pushed him off of her, then turned and headed for the bedroom. Bj walked behind her watching her ass cheeks shake twice with every step. When he entered the room, she was crawling on the bed with her ass tuted up high, then in one swift motion, she turned around and laid on her back, as she motioned for him to come with her finger.

Bj crawled on top of her and started lounging her like there's no tomorrow. He then eased his way down to her navel and then down to her mound. She arched her ass up, so he can pull her panties off. As he pulled them off her feet, she went instant into a split, so he can have nothing but a clear way to her pink clean shaved p*ssy. He went down and liked her pearl tongue a few times before turning in a sideways sixty nine position, so he can get his s*t sucked while he sucked the air out of her p*ssy. They went at it for almost 30 minutes until he shot an ounce of nut down her throat, She swallowed it all like a pro and kept on sucking. She came in his mouth the umpteenth time before he raised up and positioned himself between her legs. As soon as he enters he, her sex drive went bananas as she soaked him down with more of her juices.

"Oh sh*t! Put it all the way in! Oooh, sh*t, yeah right there. Harder baby, harder! Beat this p*ssy up!"

"Like that baby?" Bj asked as he held on to her hips while she held her legs in a Chinese split and pounded away.

"You're hitting my spot."

"This how you want it?"

"Yes! Baby, I'm coming hard Baby."

"Oh sh*t! This p*ssy good girl!"

"You like this p*ssy? Tell me you like this p*ssy."

"I like this sh*t!"

"It's your p*ssy daddy."

"I'll play second anytime daddy. Oh, oh, sh*t, I'm cumming again."

"Baby, you gone make me fall in love, baby."

Bj long stroked her until she released all her juices on his pipe. She then got on top of him with her back facing him and rode him while she made her p*ssy vibrate. He held her butt cheeks spread, while she rocked here ass back and forth.

"Oh, baby, ooh."

"Yeah, baby, I'm your bitch."

"You do what I say don't you?"

"Yes, daddy."

"I can't hear you!"

"Oh sh*t, Yes Daddy. I'm coming again, daddy. I can't take it no more. Cum with me baby." Tonya started moving faster and Bj felt his nut building to the top of his head and pulled out and shot his semen all over her butt cheeks. Tonya laid on her stomach panting and shaking as her orgasms kept flooring. She got up to go the washroom and almost fell because of her weak legs.

Bj looks at the soaking wet spot on the bed and asked, "Damn girl, how long has it been since you had some cause al this cum you left on the sheet looks like you poured a bucket of water on the bed?"

"This p*ssy stay wet all the time and don't know anybody hit this. I just let my bitches lick this."

"Yeah, why you didn't invite one over with us?

"I had to test drive first and see is anyone else worthy of sharing with me."

"So, is they?"

"I don't' think so. Anyone I catch besides your soon to be wife gone have a big problem, so be careful who you screw."

"Girl, you better be cool."

"I'm cool, just better take what I said into consideration."

"Yo' for real, though have you been on top of that info?"

"That's what I called you over here for."

"I can't tell…"

"Oh, you had that coming anyway, since you had me waiting for so long to get what I want."

"You lucky I waited and didn't kidnap you and take it!"

"Girl, please…"

"Don't under estimate me! You know my work!"

"What you got for me about dude?"

"I was in the beauty shop yesterday getting my hair done when this girl name Tricey in the other chair started showing off her jewelry to the girl who was doing her hair."

"Right."

"So she is goin on about how her man is calling the shots since dude's in the hospital' but it took her a minute to say his name until this dude walked in the shop all G'ed up and blinging like crazy. One of the girls spoke to him '____' then Tricey jumped up out of her chair saying, 'B real you better not get one of these hoe's f*cked up in here.'"

"So the n*ggas name's B Real. Yeah, so I got up to go outside to smoke a cigarette, but really to get his license plate number and I also left Monika's number on the driver side window."

"That's what's up! Did you inform her on what to do?"

"Yeah, I told her he's special, so treat him special until you get some direction."

"Girl, you on the money! I should knock your back out one more time – gorilla style."

Tonya turned around and said, "I want it doggy style."

Bj spread her ass cheeks and went straight in. Good thing as her p*ssy was still wet. The way he rammed his sh*t in her seems like it would not only hurt her, but him to. Bj went beast out for 10 minutes straight and shot his semen on her back. Tonya still had her ass up like the boss freak. She was asking for more, but Bj left her with that last bang before taking a quick shower alone and making his way home.

Bj and Sheena woke up the next morning and went looking for a house to move into. The money has been rolling in good despite all the drama that had been going on. Scrap and Pooka been operating White Boy's spot while he's been on bunk rest. Nuke also stuck to his word and had Tye, Craig and Westie bonded out. Wayne-Wayne was still on the run and no one had seen or heard from him.

Sheena and Bj found a house in Hyde Park with 2 bedrooms, a living and dining room and also a guest room. The back porch was turned into a weight/business room. From there they went to purchase some furniture and had it delivered the same day. Bj knew sh*t was starting to get real ugly as the days go on, and he had to limit himself from the people who he cared the most about to keep from bringing danger to their doorstep. He kept in touch with his mother every day through phone calls, just as he had promised and also his grandmother and aunts.

It's 10:30 am and Bj almost forgot about meeting his guys at the hall like he had planned yesterday. He hurried up and dropped Sheena off and headed to his destination.

When Bj pulled up to the Mason Hall, he saw 2 unknown cars and instantly knew it was the rental cars he had instructed Scrap and Pooka to get. One was a black 4 door Grand Prix and the other was a smoke gray Grand AM with snake tints.

When Bj walked into the hall he didn't notice the female sitting in the purple Sunfire across the street from the hall. Ever since he's been shot, he's always stayed strapped, so if things got out of hand, he could make a difference. This would be the wrong place for it do to all the artilllery that's inside the hall.

"What's up Strap and P.Dub?" Bj asked as the 3 shook hands.

"Sh*t, we waiting for you."

"What ever your call is, we with it 100%!"

"That's what I like to hear."

"Aye, yo', I got wind of who's behind all the hits that's been taken place. I'm just waiting on the full info of where he lays his head at. Does the name B. Real ring a bell?"

"B. Real, B. Real…" Scrap repeated as he tried to see where he had heard hat name from. "Oh, tha's that n*gga that run that joint on Peoria. He just copped him a Cadillac truck on 22 inch spree wells," Scrap remembered.

"Well that's the target. He's the man behind the hits. I can have my bitch Monica to take him out but I want to met with him personally," J replied.

"How you gone do that, J?" Scrap asked.

"I'm gone pop up where he at and sit down and have a talk with him and if he don't play my way then he gone die my way."

Bj and Scrap ____ was leaving the hall when Pooka noticed

the female sitting in the car across the street. "Yo, B.J, you know Shorty over there in that Sunfire? Baby girl, been sitting in that same spot since we came and every time I caught her staring."

"Naw, I don't know Shorty. What about you Scrap?" Bj asked.

"Me neither, but I'm bout to find out!" Scrap said as he headed across the street in her direction. She panicked and pulled off, but not before Scrap got a chance to get a look at her license plate.

Bj called Tonya and gave her the license plate number and told her to get back with him on the info ASAP. Bj went on, "Tonya tell Shorty M to get my man to the club and let one know, so I can have a sit down and talk to him."

"Alright Bj I'm gone call you back in thirty."

"Aye, Tonya, I need all that done ASAP."

"I got you Bj.!"

Tonya called Bj back with the info he had asked for, "the girl in the Sunfire is named ShaMeaka Ford. Do you know her J.?"

"Naw, I don't know her."

"JB.. I asked Monica for the license plates to B Real's truck and it comes back to the same person. "Cause I feel if she's spying and y'all into with B Real, then maybe they have some type of connection."

"That's why I like you girl, cause you think for the unthinkable!"

"Boy, stop! And Bj Monica told B Real that her best friend is having a birthday party at the Tom River Center and he's

104

going to be there."

"Perfect timing! Get about five of your girls ready to party tonight, just in case he don't take my offer. Then we gone get it popin in that bitch, but I hope it don't go down like that."

"B. J. we gone need more than the ladies cause this cat don't go nowhere without a whole entourage."

"I'm already on top of that. Just make sure you girls are heated cause they don't search the females. You know where to get the heat from and be careful when you come and go cause there's nosy people – whose nose been running around here."

"Alright J., I'll see you at 10 tonight."

"No doubt!"

"Aye Scrap and Pooka get Team RedRum together and have them to secure the club tonight with a 2 block radius and wait for my word. It's about to go down tonight, but I want you two in the club with me and make sure y'all vest up. He picked the right fight, but with the wrong people."

Bj and his guys rode around the club in the Grand Am that they had rented earlier. On every corner in a 2 block radius was one of his guys from Teams Red and Rum and one was parked directly across the street from the club with a clear view of who ever would come or go.

Bj pulled up in one of the VIP parking spaces and got out. A shuffer boy was there to take his keys, although he passed on the offer of service, he still gave the guy a $100 bill. When they arrived at the door, the two 6'7" bouncers acknowledged them and moved the rope for them to enter in without paying or being searched.

Once inside the club, they looked around to check the surroundings before heading to a VIP table in the corner. This table was prime, as there is not a lot of light. Once they were seated, a waitress arrived with a bucket of ice and 2 bottles of Rose Moet in it and 3 glasses – all courtesy of the owner, who is a close friend of his brother, Nuke. Bj put a $50 bill in her bra then smacked her on the ass as she walked away.

Ten minutes later Tonya arrived at the table dressed in an all black cat suit that looked like it was painted on her.

"Is everything set?" Bj asked.

"Yes, all the girls is set up throughout the club, They are aware of your every move. They been watching you since you steeped foot in the club."

How do I know who they are?"

"Cause they all have on the same thing as me, except that each one of them have caramel skins and has a long black pony tail."

"OK, I see one of them over there. Is our guest here yet?"

"NO, he's not her but I just got a call that they are on their way in a silver Land Cruiser, "Tonya reported.

"Aye, Scrap locate Team Red Rum and let them know what kind of truck to have on their radar and tell them not to move tilll they hear Mona Lisa." Bj ordered.

"I got you," Scrap shot back.

"Aye Tonya, try to stay away from me for the rest of the night cause you got me ready to break my vows."

"Boy, please be serious."

"Naw, for real though, I want you to go and say something

to each one of the ladies, so I can know their exact spot cause I only see 2 of them."

"Alright."

As Tonya was walking off, Meaka came walking past her towards Bj's table. Tonya sized her up trying to figure out where she knew her from, but kept on going to do what she was told.

"What's up Mr. Don't' want no more of this good p*ssy?"

"Is that all you think about is getting f*cked?"

"Well, if it's you who's going to be f*cking me, then yeah."

"Yeah. Quit it with the bull shit. What's up? What you want a drink or something?"

"Naw, I want to know why you ain't been answering my phone calls."

"Well, since you want to know, I'm engaged now, and I don't' cheat."

"A huh, by who?"

"All that don't matter, but do you mind excusing yourself? I'm waiting on someone and I don't want to start a conversation

"Well, I want to know can I get one more night with you?"

"Meaka, it was only a one night thing. Shorty, I told you that."

"You gone stunt on me like…"

The DJ yelled over the speaker, "to give a shout out to the one and only B Real," as he walked through the door and when Bj turned back around, Meaka was gone.

"Looking for someone ?" Tonya asked.

"Tonya, I thought she still right here," Bj said.

"I see she had you distracted that you didn't even pay attention to the order you gave me."

"You're right and I'm sorry."

"Do you know her?"

"Yeah, I know her from somewhere but I can't pout my finger on it."

"Her name is Meaka and I met her through my brother when I got out of jail."

"That's where I know her from! When you have me to run her license plate today and B Real's truck is in her name."

"That scandalous bitch! Tonya, do you know she just asked me to sleep with her one last time cause I told her I was engaged?"

"You just give me the word and you know what time it is."

"Naw, we got something else in store for her. Let me get on over here to dude and you go on before someone see me talking to you and our cover gets blown."

"Alright Bj but I got my eye on you just give me a wink."

"I'm sorry Tonya, but go let me know where everyone at one more time, so I would know before I walk over there."

After Tonya went around the room one more time, Bj, Scrap and Pooka walked over to the VIP section where B Real was. They couldn't get directly to him because of the body guard and his entourage.

"Who y'all want?" was what one of the guards said.

"I want to speak to B Real," Bj spoke.

Before the guard could say another word, B Real yelled to

let him through but his boys had to wait on the other side of that line.

Bj responded, "All due respect B Real. I'm a man of authority and they with me, so if I'm welcome then they're welcome."

Before Bj could speak, two of B Real's guys popped off, "Who is this clown, B Real?"

Scrap spoke up before Bj could say anything, "Ain't no need for the name calling slick homie. We just here to talk but we ain't ducking no trouble."

"B Real, just give me the word," the guy reminded him.

"Hold on fellas, y'all causing unwanted attention."

"Bj we need to set a date at another time but right now we getting our party on and y'all blowing our high."

B Real raised up like he was ready to fight, so Bj stepped backward and said, "You know what? We will meet again. Come brothers, let's go."

"Yeah, y'all better ride before it be some thing in here," was what the loud-mouthed guy with B Real added.

Bj turned in Tonya's direction and nodded his head as he was walking toward the front exit. Tonya got on her phone to let Monica know to move from the crowd. When she stepped from the crowd, Tonya and her crew approached the crowd in the VIP section, which was full of thirsty n*ggas and joined the party. B Real flagged down the waitress and signaled for her to bring 5 bottles of Rose Monet. Tonya stared dancing in he middle of e the crowd and everyone was focused on her as she danced to R Kelly's song, "Move Your Body Like a Snake." Then all of a sudden gun shots broke out in the VIP section, as the girls begun to blaze the guys up. Instead of them trying to run out of the VIP section, they all dove to cover B Real. Tonya backed up out of the VIP section firing the 2 nines that she had in her hand, so that they can exit out the side door close to where they were. People starting running everywhere out front trying to get to their cars or anywhere out of the line of fire. Monica, the get away driver, was waiting in the truck out back for Tonya and the ladies. Team RedRum stood on point waiting for the word for them to finish things, while the girls were exiting.

Ten to fifteen of B Real's guys were laid out in the VIP section, the 2 body guards along with five of B Real's guys ran out the front door with B Real in the middle of their crowd.

Bj and his guys watched as B Real limped to the passenger side of his truck. One of the guards jumped in the driver's seat and pulled off.

Scrap asked Bj to give hi the word, but Bj told him that he got a better plan for him. ""Call Team RedRum and tell them that we're out but one of them is to follow his truck and see where he's going."

On that noise, Nuke yelled as the Channel 9 news lady came on, "We have a breaking news story right now. Shots broke out in a night club about 30 minutes ago. We believe that six females opened fire on about 20 something men in a VIP section inside this club. The guard says they don't know how the ladies got inside with the guns because everyone is searched on their way inside. Sixteen people were shot, six dead, five seriously wounded and the other four, I mean the other five have minor in and out wounds. Police have the club blocked off while they investigate more. Some witnesses say that there were men doing the shooting, but one of the people who was shot inside the VIP section confirmed that it was all females. We will try to get you some more info as the investigation goes on. This is Lisa Marie, form Channel 9 news. Back to you, Stacy."

"Hell, naw, them hoes got it crackin in the Rom River Center. Joe, I wonder who they was?" one of the guys yelled out of his chuck hole in his cell door.

The next morning, Nuke called his brother to try and get more info on what went on at the club. He's been hearing a lot about sh*t going on out there, but hasn't been able to talk to his brother, because of his visits only being once a week and today is his first visiting day and his lil brother isn't answering his phone.

The guard came on the deck calling out names for visits, "Jose Chavas, Jason Roberts, Demarcus Barker, Deante Proul and Reggie Anderson, y'all have a visit". Everyone who was called walked up to the door to be searched before they were allowed to leave the deck for their visit.

When Nuke walked in the visiting room, Bj was sitting at the glass waiting for him to sit down.

"What's up big bro?" Bj asked.

"What's up with you out there?"

"Is everything going swell out there?"

"Yeah the money stilll rollin' in but it's wartime right now."

"Is that your work I've been hearing about?"

"Naw, that's they work."

111

"White Boy get out the hospital tomorrow."

"Yeah, is he cool?"

"Yeah, he cool."

"You know bout 5 days ago I got shot in the side but it went in and out without f*cking sh*t up."

"Lil bro, you got to be careful out there. I'm going to go crazy if I hear some thing happened to you."

"I'm cool, big bro. I'm a soldier. That sh*t on the news was my work. I got Tonya to put a team of girls together, so my hands stay clean."

"Who you warring with?"

"You ever heard of B Real?"

"Yeah, that's Tear Drop's right hand man."

"Well, he's the one who's been sending all the hits my way. So last night, I tried to talk to him at the club to squash the beef, but he tried to stunt on me like he's the man in charge, so I back up off him and left the club. Then sh*t went wild, so they can't say I had sh*t to do with it."

"Did they get they target?"

"Naw, but we know where he rest his head at, so we on top of that."

"Lil bro, watch out cause dude is grimy. so gone get him out the way before he slip up and get lucky."

"I got you but what that broyer talking about?"

"He saying I'm probably gone have to sit bout 3 months before he can get me a bond. He says his wife and the judge wife been friends for a long time, so I'm chillin."

"OK. Have Tiff to hit me up if she or you need anything. I

bought me and Sheena a house, you know. I proposed to her. I didn't feel right staying at the crib and you wasn't there."

"You know what's mine is your."

"I know but I just didn't feel right."

"How's mom doing?"

"She cool. We talk over the phone a lot since sh*t been hectic. You feel me?"

"Yeah, I feel you but I'm gone let you gone get out of here. Be safe out there. Love lil bro."

"Always big bro, love."

"Aye, Tonya, everything cool on your end?"

"Yeah, everything cool. I got the girls with me and so far the police don't know nothing, but that it was some girls."

"That's what's up. Have you heard from Monica?"

"Yeah, I just got off the phone with her earlier, She say she called dude and confronted him about leaving her at the club."

"Yeah, is they still cool?"

"She said yeah, but she got him thinking that she still mad at him."

"That's cool, cause I need here away from him for a few days."

"I'm on top of that boo."

"Aye, Tonya, White Boy gets out in the morning. I need you to send one of your girls who crib he can lay up in for a few days to go get him."

"Alright, is there anything else you need done?"

"Naw, that's it for right now."

Bj, Scarppy and Pooka rode around in the other rental car looking for B Real. They been by both of his cribs and even through his hood. Pooka yelled up to the front seat for Bj to pull into Burger King's drive thru . As they were bout to pull in Meaka comes out the door with some dude holding their food. Bj turned his had the other way, as they rode past her, so she won't see who he is.

Bj pulled to the back and made a u-turn, so he can get behind her and follow them. Bj stayed 2 car lengths behind her and followed them all the way to the east side. Once they reached her block, he parked on the corner, while she parked in the middle of he block. Meaka got out and walked up to this 2 flat building and inserted her key in the door on the first floor and both of them went in.

Thirty minutes later, Bj sent Pooka and Scrap to the back door, while he went to the front door. He knocked on he door and waited for her to answer. Meaka came to the door and asked "who is it?"

"It's Bj," he replied. "Oh, you don't know who I am now?"

Meaka finally recognized his voice and opened the door.

Bj figured the dude must be somewhere in the back cause he couldn't see anyone when she opened the door.

"What you want and how you know where I stay?"

"Meaka, I need to use your phone. It's important! The police just chased me 4 blocks from here and I seen you going in the house, but I couldn't come out from under the car cause I didn't know where they was..." Bj rattled. It sounded like some bull sh*t. "Girl, I'm for real. What you gone do? Leave me out here to get caught?"

Meaka replied, "I got company in here, so you gone have to wait till I go get my phone."

"Hurry up.,. before they pull up!"

Meaka turned around to go get her phone and left the door cracked open. Before she could make it fully into the house, Bj had his gun out and aimed at the back of her head. "Bitch, don't move or say a word or I would blow your f*cking brains out."

Bj called Scrap's cell phone and told him to come around the front and come in. When both Scrap and Pooka were in, Bj signaled for them to go get dude from out the back.

When Scrap and Pooka returned to the front room with the guy, Bj had Meaka on the floor naked with only her panties on. He used her bra to tie her hands behind her back. "Tie his ass up too and put him in one of those chairs."

After Meaka and dude were tied up in the chairs, Bj took the floor. "Right now, y'all life depend on the truth. But let me tell v'all one thing and that's to keep in mind how much I know already, so when you lie you feel pain and if you lie to much then you die. Hey, I like that rhyme. I should be a rapper." Bj started singing, "You lie, you , you , you die. You lie, you, you , you…"

Scrap and Pooka started cracking up.

Bj continued, "I hop y'all feel where I'm coming from. First off, slick homie, where you from? and before you answer remember, if you lie what happens. Tell me what happens if you lie?"

115

"I die"

"Good boy. This gone be easy and everybody lives. Now answer my question – where you from?"

"I'm from 58th and Carpenter."

"So you know who Tear Drop is right?"

"Yeah"

"What is your relation with dude?"

"I work for his right hand man.

"And who is that?"

"B Real."

"I like this guy here fellas. He knows how to listen and follow directions. What is your relations with B Real?

"I'm his cousin."

"I know. and you know how I know? You look like his bitch ass."

Now Meaka, I hope you been paying attention as well as you like creeping, if you know what I'm talking about. "I take it that you know B Real as well, right? How well do you know him, Meaka?" Bj said as he turned his attention to the other chair.

"I slept with him a couple of times, only a couple of times. Yeah, that's it." she responded.

"When was the last time y'all was together?"

"About 3 weeks ago."

Smack.

Bj slapped the shit out of Meaka. "Now, I'm gonna ask you again, when was the last time y'all was together?"

"Two days ago," Meaka said through the sniffles from the

slap that sent tears to her eyes.

"Why was you watching me on Ashland the other day?"

"He made me cause he knew we had messed around before."

"Oh, you told him that?"

"Yeah, why?"

"Cause he said if I let him know your every move that he would pay me."

"So is that why you asked me to spend the night with you the other night?"

"NO, I wanted to let you know what he had me doing and then we can get at him and take everything he has."

"You a scandalous bitch! You don't care who you trade on as long as you come up!"

"Bryant, I love you!"

"Bitch, you love this dick. Do B Real know that you're f*cking his lil cousin?"

"No, cause it ain't his business."

"Oh, yeah, well this what we gone do. We gone call B Real and invite him over."

"Please don't do this."

"Bitch, shut up hoe. It's gone be three n*ggas that done stuck dick in you in one house, then I might let my boys see what it do."

Scrap said, "Naw. I'm cool."

Pooka added "Me too."

"We gone call him up off your phone and tell him to come over – it's important," Bj ordered.

"B Real, I need you to come over to my house, it's very important and I can't talk over the phone," Meaka said.

"Meaka, you better not be on bullshit," was B Real's reply.

"I swear to God, it's important!"

"OK, Meaka, I'll be over there in an hour."

"Hurry up!"

"I just told you I'll be over there."

After Meaka hung up the phone, Bj told them that one of them was goin to live and one of them was going to die. "Because one of y'all gone have to tell B Real my message and the one that's dead is gone be the showing of my message. Now, I'm gone give y'all a few seconds to decide who gone to live and who's gonna die."

Bj turned around to Scrap and mumbled something, then turned back around to Meaka and the other cat in the chair. "Time's up," he announced.

Pooka was standing behind Meaka and stuffed a sock in her mouth, so she wouldn't scream while watching Scrap cut the other guy's neck from ear to ear.

"Now, Meaka, when B Real shows up, tell him that this his last chance to get a message to me saying he's willing to speak with me on my terms and my terms only or he's gonna wish he died in his sleep and not feel the wrath that's coming his way." Bj Turned around to leave, and then turned back towards Meaka and said, "Oh, one more thing, this is your warning also. Don't cross me or cross my path in the wrong way or you will be next. So the next time and I know after B Real see this, he's gonna have another job for you. If it's aiming towards me, you better take him out for trying to send you at me. Let's go fellas and wipe those door knobs off on the way out."

B Real arrived at Meaka's house with 2 cars full of his guys. He seen Meaka's car parked in front of her house, so he figured she was there. He signaled for 2 of his mans to get out of the car and make sure everything was cool and it wasn't no set up waiting for him. He knew a thirsty female like Meaka will do anything for some money, so he was being careful.

After the 2 guys checked the gang ways and the cars that was close by, B Real exited his car and went up to her door and knocked. He didn't get an answer, so he knocked even harder and the door came open. He jumped back cause he wasn't expecting the door to be unlocked. When he peeked in, he saw Meaka tied up in a chair and another person next to her with his head leaning down and blood all over his neck and shirt.

He pointed for this 2 guys to enter first and secure the house. Once the house was secure, B Real entered and found that the other person was his cousin sitting in that chair with his throat split from ear to ear. "OH tell me it isn't Rico! Tell me it ain't!"

B Real snatched the sock from out of Meaka's mouth and spazed out on her, "Bitch, who did this?"

"Bj and two of his guys ran in here. I swear to God, B Real, I didn't have nothing to do with it. He told me to tell you this is your last chance to speak with him on his terms and his terms only or you gonna wish you died in your sleep and not feel the wrath from him," Meaka blurted in one breath.

119

"Oh, yeah, so he want to play for keeps. Right, I swear to God that he picked the right one to f*ck with. Clean this shit up and get Ricoup out of here." He started walking to the door and Meaka yelled afer him, "Ain't you gonna untie me, B Real?"

He turned and ordered his guys to untie her and looked her in the eye and said, "Bitch you have 2 days to have me some information on him or someone in his family or you're going to be the next one being buried."

"Yes, I'm here to pick up Jamal Jones," Sherell said to the lady at the front desk of Menard Hospital.

"He's in room 202 getting dressed. You can go help him if you want to," was the courteous reply.

"Thanks, very much."

As Sherell entered the room, White Boy was pulling his pants up and thought it was one of the nurses entering the room. "Can you get my prescription, so I can get up out of this sick place?" he asked.

"Don't be so rude to these people. They're only here to help you," Sherell shot back.

"Who is your sexy, walking in my room?"

"I'm Sherell and I was sent to pick you up and let's just say cater to your needs."

"I think I'm goin to like this task."

"Well, you will be staying with me for a while and if you're as nice as they say you are, I might not let you go."

"Well, baby girl you might as well put on a harness cause it's gone be a long ride."

120

"I like the way that sounds!"

B Real rode around contemplating on a way to get back at Bj. He realized that the stakes had just been raised to a higher level and he'd have to really be more careful or he would end up like Tear Drop or worse. He then realized that he's the only one that's allowed to see Tear Drop besides his mother and it's been almost a month since he's been to check up on him. He calls Monica to escort him to the hospital, as she's the only one he feels he can trust.

"What's up sweetie?" was the answer.

He asks, "Are you still mad at me, Monica?"

"Yeah, a little, but I kind of been sick so I didn't want to be bothered with anyone."

"Why didn't you call me to come help you heal?"

"Cause I was only sick, but I was also on my you know what and when you're around me, it's like I just stay wet and horny. I took some time for myself."

"Look, boo, I need to go see my man at this hospital and you're the only one I trust right now, since all this bullshit been happening and plus its only me and his mom that's allowed to visit him. You might have to stay in the lobby or the car."

"So, you want me to ride with you just to stay in the car or lobby? I don't think so."

"Please boo! I really need you right now."

Monica thought about what he had just asked her. She changed her mind, "OK, I'm at my sister's crib on 83rd and Loomis. Call me when you get close."

121

Monica called Tonya and told her about the conversation that she had just had with B Real. Tonya told her to try her best to get as much info as she can and to call her every time she's alone.

Monica was sitting outside when B Real called her so he wouldn't know exactly where she was staying. Out of all the times that they been seeing each other, she never let him know where she was staying. They always either meet up somewhere or when they spelt together, they would go to one of his houses or a hotel. She would always tell him that her mother was a Jehovah's Witness and that she wouldn't allow any males into her home unless they were one too.

Monica hopped in the rental car that B Real was driving and gave him a hug and a kiss to show how much she had missed him. She wouldn't dare blow the chance of getting the info that this whole task of being with B Real in the first place.

B Real and Monica arrived in front of St Colombus Hospital, B Real paid the door clerk to park in the garage. When they walked up to the desk, B Real was a little hesitant at first but went on anyway."I'm here to see Thomas Diver, please."

"What is your name, sir?" the nurse asked.

"Byron Davis."

"Can I please see some ID or driver's license sir, with your picture on it?" she asked.

He handed her his driver's' license and she looked at it and handed it back to him. She then asked if Monica was with him, but Monica said she would wait in the lobby. The nurse gave him a visiting pass and told him that Thomas was in room 110 straight ahead.

Bj, White Boy, Scrap and Pooka were sitting at Sherell's house out eat playing the video game and listening to the radio. Sherell came in with a tray full of submarine sandwiches and a pitcher of orange juice. "Here's some lunch for you guys, especially Mr. Cause you gone need some weight on you to handle me," she said to White Boy.

The fellas started laughing and pointing at White Boy. Sherell turned around to walk off and White Boy slapped her on her ass little hard and she jumped and started rubbing her butt. "Well, I really see what way I'm going to have to apologize Miss Lady." White Boy offered.

White Boy got up and turned the game off, so they could talk about what's been going on while he was in the hospital and to see if his guys have something planned for B Real and his crew.

"Aye bro-bro, what we gone do to knock these cats off so it want be no back and forth shit keep going on, before one of us end up getting killed."

"You know I can have Monica to take him out at anytime, but what type of man am I to have a female to do my work? We're leaders not cheaters!"

"I live for the action and he's gonna die by my gun and my gun only."

"I feel you bro, but we don't need to be stalling. Let's gone get him out of the way, so we can shoot our paper to the limit."

"Ain't nothing wrong with our money flow. Your strip being

doing lovely. Pooka and Scrap been doing the damn thang out there. So when you get fully healthy, I'm gone let them open up there own strip where ever they want."

"Scarp and PDub, I appreciate y'all for helping me out while I'm down," White Boy said gratefully.

"No problem, bro. We family. We did that cause that's the love we got for you," Scrap said.

"Yeah bro, that's what love we got for you and we know you would do the same for us," Pooka added.

"You damn right I would!"

"Aye fellas, check this out right – we just got word of where that bitch ass n*gga T Drop laying up at, so we gone go see Nuke on his visiting day and see how he wants to take care of dude and if he wants us to take him out. That way it's done for him and B Real the easy way, but I really want B Real myself and I won't feel right by letting a

"Naw. he's stilll in the hospital. We just know which one he's in now and Tonya say we got a couple of people on the inside, but not one that takes care of him. She's working on that."

"OK, bro, I'm with you 70% for right now, but in a few days, I'll be fully revcovered at 100% and n*ggas gone feel it," White Boy added.

Phil aka Andre Barker is Nuke and Bj's older cousin. He's not a street n*gga but he has been playing basketball in the C.B.U. league for four years now. He was at Washington Park playing basketball for $1,000 a game. The score was 12-9 his way. B Real and his guys was side betting against Phil with some cats that was up there watching the game also. "Aye T Mac, you better not let that sucker beat you or you gone be paying me my money back."

"If you think I'm a sucker, then put on you some shorts and get next."

The crowd started "ooh" and "ahh" B Real got up and stopped the game.

"Listen here bitch ass n*gga, you better watch who the f*ck you talking to before I end you career."

"Look homie, you must not know who my people's is or you wouldn't be talking that shit out your mouth."

"I wouldn't give a f*ck who your people's is, n*gga."

"My cousin's Nuke and Bj run this shit around here."

"Oh, them your people's?"

"Yeah, them my people's n*gga!"

"Oh, my fault bro, I don't want no problems with you and your peoples."

Phil and T Mac continued their game and the score is 15-14 game point. Phil way, phil check T Mac, the ball and when T Mac was about to check it back, four masked men ran on the court with their guns pointed at Phil and walked him over to an all black mini van and pulled off. T Mac was happy cause he knew he was about to lose and didn't know how he was going to pay B Real.

Bj was on his way home when his cell phone started ringing. He looked at the caller ID and saw that it was his cousin Phil's number, so he answered it, "What's up Mr. CBA when you gone be in town?"

An unfamiliar voice spoke, "He's already in town, the question is where is he?"

"Who's this that I'm talking to?"

"I'm in control mother f*cker, so stop asking questions and listen. This B Real and I have your smart mouth ass cousin. I see he didn't know about our little altercation or he wouldn't told me that he was your peoples and he wouldn't be sitting here hog tied to this table bout to go through surgery while he's woke. OOW, so painful."

"You lay one hand on him B Real and I swear to God…"

"You might as well leave God out of this as you can hear him in the background screaming like a bitch, yeah that's him."

Bj sat on the other end of the phone quiet as he heard his cousin screaming, "Aye Bj, you still with me ain't you?"

" This what I'm gone do since you wanted to involve family members, you gone get his body, but I hope he wasn't an organ donor cause I'm feeding all that to my dog. He hasn't ate in three weeks. I'll call yo later with the address where his body gone be and I advise you to think twice before you f*ck with me. You can't win."

"You gonna wish…"

"Before Bj could finish his words the phone went dead.

Bj called Pooka and Scrap and told them to meet him at the Mason Hall but to come in through the back.

When Scrap and Pooka walked in, they knew instantly by the look on Bj's face that something was wrong and that there

126

about to be some more blood shedding and a lot of it. "Yo, what happen, bro?" Scrap said to break the tension.

"This bitch ass n*gga, B Real, done kidnapped Phil and got him somewhere torturing him as we speak," Bj opened.

"How he get Phil?"

"He was somewhere playing ball and him and somebody had some words and he told dude that he's my cousin and were not to be f*cked with and that's when B Real had him kidnapped, I swear to God that he's bout to feel me real hard. I mean super hard. When I finish with him, they gone think he was lynched by the same white boys that lynched Emit Tilll." Bj replied.

"Let's go get his ass now."

"Naw, we have to wait to he calls to let me know where the body at. I at least have to get my cousin's body back, so I can bury him the right way."

Two days done pass and there still has not been any word from B Real about where Phil's body was at, so now Bj starts getting inpatient and ready to go find B Real and tear him a new ass hole, but he gets a call from Nuke asking him if he is coming to visit him today. He's so unfocused that he forgot that his brother's visiting day was today. "Yeah, I'm on my way up there. Now, there's a lot of shit I need to talk to you about."

"Alright, I'll see you when you get up here."

"Alright, love."

"You too lil bro."

Bj was just getting out of the car in front of the county jail when he heard his phone start ringing. He reached under the seat

127

to grab it, then it stopped. He was about to set it back down when it started ringing again. He looked at the caller ID and saw it was a restricted number and knew it was the call he was waiting for.

"Hello," Bj said in an aggressive tone.

"Sorry to keep you waiting so long but this bitch ass cousin of you're a fighter cause he wouldn't give me any information I wanted about you or your family."

"Let's stop the bullshit and tell me where I need to go to get the body from."

"That's no way to talk to a person who got something that belongs to you that you want dearly."

"Let's see how bad you want your cousin's body back…"

"I thought you was gonna…"

"Hold up lil homie, you don't get paid for thinking. Let me do the thinking for you from now on and you won't have to worry about being in this position or the position that your cousin's in, well, was in. But since I'm a man of my word cause that's all I owe you, I'm gonna send the body to you for free, but I advise you not to f*ck with me anymore. You hear me?"

Bj didn't respond.

"I said do you hear me?"

"Yeah, I heard you."

"His body gonna be in the trunk of this car in the back of that church on 55th and Paulina. I did pray for him before I left him there. Ha, ha, ha," as B Real hangs up the phone.

Bj hopped back in the car and headed to the location that B Real just gave him. He called Scrap and told him where the body was located and don't do nothing till he gets there.

128

When Bj made it there, it was so many policemen around, and the area was taped off from one end of the alley to the other one. Scrap walked up to Bj and told him that when he got there that everything was going on already and that some bum was walking through the alley and was trying to break in the trunk and that's when he saw the body and called the police.

:Sir, that is my cousin over there. Can you tell me what morgue y'all talking him to, so I can have my aunt to come identify his body," Bj asked one of the officers.

The officer responds with, "Excuse me sir, what's your name?"

"That don't even matter officer."

"Can you tell me the victim's name?"

"It's Andre Barker."

"Sir, do you have any idea who would want to hurt him?"

"No sir, but if you find out can you let me know?"

Bj called his Auntie Joann as he was walking away from the crime scene and let her know what had happened. She asked him to come pick her up, but instead he sent his girl Sheena, as he didn't want to see his aunt so hurt.

When he went back to the county jail he had to run in because it was 8:20 pm and if you're not there by 8:30, you are not able to visit. When he made it to the visiting cage, Nuke looked like he had an attitude because the last time he had talked to Bj, was 3 hours earlier. Why was he just now making it here to see him??

"What's up lil bro? What took you so long to get up here? I talked to you about 3 or 4 hours ago and you said you was on your way."

"Aye, Phil was kidnapped 2 days ago and I been waiting for a call to let me know where the body was at. B Real and his guys grabbed him off the court, " Bj said.

"What made them grab him? They don't know him."

"He had got into it with somebody out there on the court and you know how he is, always putting our names out there and so happened B Real was already looking for me supposedly cause I just got down on his lil cousin, so he call this retaliation, but was on my way here to see you. I had to detour as soon as I got out of my car the phone started ringing and it was dude bitch ass telling me where he left the body."

"What's with this cat, B Real? You have to stop the kiddie shit with this n*gga and play for keeps before you end up getting hurt out there. I know you got an easy way to get him out of the way without getting your hands dirty."

"See that's the problem. I want this n*gga myself and I won't feel right if I have someone else to do it."

"Sometimes we have to take the easy way so we can be out on the streets to keep making the way."

"Aye, big bro, you know we just got the info on where dude at."

"Dude who?"

Tear Drop."

"Yeah, is he still active?"

"Naw, I thin he's still f*cked up, but we will know for sure before this week is out."

"What you want us to do with him?"

"Don't worry about him yet, just handle what you got going with this other cat then get back at me about dude."

"Wrap them visits up in 2 minutes fellas," the officer shouted.

"This visit about to be over, but keep your head up out there and stop playing with them n*ggas and gone get them out the way. I'm goine be calling you soon so be expecting my call."

"I'm always waiting on your call, big bro."

"Alright, I'm gone holla at your later, lil bro, love."

"Right, love."

Bj left the county jail with vengeance on his mind. He know what his brother was saying was true, but he still felt that it was his job to handle B Real himself cause of the disrespect he pushed him away.

Bj called Tonya and told her that he needed to meet her within the next hour. Tonya thought about seeing if she could get her a couple of nuts off in the process, but changed her mind due to the tone and eagerness in Bj's voice, sounded only like business and business only.

Tonya was sitting in the Cheesecake Factory downtown waiting on Bj and his guys to arrive. The waitress came up to the table and asked her if she was ready to order yet. She told the waitress to get her a fresh cup of orange juice and a glass of water.

"Will that be it,, mam?" the waitress asked.

"You can call me Tonya. What's your name?" Tonya asked.

"It's Sharice."

"I like that name, Sharice," Tonya said with a little flirtation in her voice. "Do you mind if I ask where you are from?"

"I'm sorry Tonya, but I'm not allowed to mingle while I', at work."

"Ok, then when you come back with my orange juice, I'll have my number ready for you to call me when your shift is over."

Sharice was at a loss for words because she had never had a woman come at her so strong and very confident about what they wanted. She smiled as she walked off. Tonya knew she nailed her in her pocket.

Bj, White Boy, Scrap and Pooka arrived at the restaurant and joined Tonya at her table. When they were seated, the waitress returned to ask the fellas what they would be ordering. They each made their order and then started on the problem at hand. Tonya passed the waitress a piece of paper before she walked off. The guys looked at the transaction, as if they was lost or something.

"Don't worry fellas. She has just joined my team," Tonya announced.

"Shorty, you stay coming up, don't you?"

"Yeah, but that's for us,"

Pooka said, "Who is us, cause I want to be first?"

"Naw, boo, not all of us just three, me, her and my daddy," she said as she looked at Bj.

"Let's get to what's going on right now. When all this shit is over, we gone have a big orgy, with 30 females and just the four of us. Then, I'm through. I'm going to get married," Bj said.

"This is what's happening, Tonya. B Real got ahold of one of my cousins and took him out in the rawest form and I'm tired of this back and forth shit. I need as much info about him as possible. I want to know where his mother stay, is father, his sister, his right hand man, his dog , his cat, his everything, and I mean EVERYTHING. He done crossed the line when he f*cked with my family. I want you to put some of your girls that's not been in the limelight and send them out to find out as much as they can. I know Monica should be able to find out any and everything about his family and I need this like yesterday."

Bj continued, "I also need you to book a 3 week cruise for five, so I can get my loved ones away cause this about to be a bloody month and I mean its bout to be a flood of nothing but blood. The news gone call it 'Bloodsnamie'".

Everyone looked at him like he lost his mind, but knew he was serious and that B Real done brought out the demon in a church full of non-believers.

B Real and his guys were sitting in his basemenet playing video games and shooting pool. J Hood, who is B Real's right hand, says, "B Real what's up with your girl Monica? You know my birthday is in 2 days. I know she got a lot of freaky ass friends. Let's throw a hotel party or something."

"That's a good idea, Hood, " one of the other guys chimed in.

B Real just stood there listening as all the fellas went on and on about what they gone do an how off the chain the party was gone be.

When they were finished, B Real stepped in, "While y'all got y'all hands on y'all dicks, and going on and on about some bitches, y'all forgot it's a war zone going on out here and that's a good place to get all of us at one time with our pants down. Them hoes gone be here now and when we dead and gone, our money flow is showing some small numbers now. Our territory is getting taken over by the enemy. Our men is dying and all y'all care about is some p*ssy in a hotel. Y'all some stupid ass n*ggas. In fact, get the f*ck out my crib. Y'all lost your f*cking minds!"

Everyone started leaving before B Real really started to act a fool. When he's mad he looses his mind. He would start throwing pool balls and hitting n*ggas with pool cues. Shit one time he started shooting in the crib because two of his men started fighting and knocked over his glass table and smashed his 32" flat screen.

J Hood was still sitting there as if he wasn't talking to him. B Real turns and asks, "What the f*ck you waiting on n*gga? You the one that came up with that bullshit. I'm highly upset with you personally. You supposed to be my right hand man. You supposed to be thinking when I'm off my square. I think you need to take you a ride and get you some fresh air, cause I'm not feeling you right now!"

"I'm cool, bro. I just fell off my square."

"Naw, you need to go get you some fresh air, like I said."

J Hood saw the look on B Real's face and got up to leave, as he did, he spoke, "I'll hit you up later."

134

"Then, that's what you do. Aye, J Hood when you get your head straight, get our squad together cause I know Bj is plotting to retaliate and I want to be ready."

"Hello mother. How you been doing?"

"Fine, I just been worrying about you out there in them streets."

"I'm fine ma. I was calling you to let you know that I booked a cruise of you, Sheena, Grandma and the rest of your sisters for 3 weeks. I'm paying for everything. The cruise starts Monday, so you need to call the rest of them and tell them to start packing."

"Boy, why you didn't let me know ahead of time. You know I just can't up and leave work for 3 weeks. I have to take care of them folks 5 days a week."

"Ma, I got some one to cover you tilll you get back, so start packing and I'm gone send a limo to pick you and the rest of them up and have y'all on the plane by 10:00 tonight."

"Boy, I'm gone hurt you for this."

"Ma, just pack up. I love you!"

White Boy and Pooka were riding up 47th and Ashland, then they noticed a black bronco pulling out the parking space in front of Footlocker. The driver made a u-turn and that's when Pooka noticed the driver as one of ht en*ggas that was at the club with B Real.

"Y'all that's them n*ggas that we got into it with at the club. That' that same truck dude_____ was is that blazed me up."

White Boy made a u-turn and sped up in the Taurus he had rented to catch up with the bronco. He passed Pooka his Desrt eagle to put one in the chamber. Pooka did so, then made sure he had one in his Glock 45. As they got up behind the truck, they tried to get on the side of them but the bronco wouldn't let them. White Boy pulled all the way into the other lane facing the oncoming traffic to be able to get along side and let a few shots off into the driver's side of the car.

As soon as he made it on the side of them, shots came from the bronco into the windshield and the passenger door of the Taurus. White Boy was forced to ease on the brakes in order to get out of traffic and also out of the line of fire. Pooka hung out the passenger window letting off shots into the back window of the bronco. The guys in the bronco ducked for cover. White Boy was able to get on the side of the bronco and hit the driver up. He let off 5 shots into the driver's door, while Pooka aimed at the windows. One of the shots must have hit the driver cause he lifted up just enough for Pooka to hit him twice in the face. The driver leaned towards the left, which made him ram White Boy from the side then the bronco bounced back to the right and slammed into a parked car. White Boy kept on going as he looked into the rearview mirror at the crime scene behind him. When he put his eyes back on the road, it was a police car heading towards him head on. He swerved to the left missing the police car by an inch. The officer made a u-turn and went for the chase. White Boy made a right on 53rd and stopped at the alley blocking it off, so that no cars can get past him, while he and Pooka hopped out and ran up the alley and went through a gang way towards Marshfield. By the time the squad car made it in view of the Taurus, all they saw were the open doors and an empty car. They looked through the alley and didn't see anyone. they tried Marshfield and still came up short. All the guys that were standing on the corner just looked at the officers like they were crazy. The officers returned to bag up the Taurus and waited for the forensics to come take ballistics and fingerprints. White Boy and Pooka hid 3 blocks over waiting for their ride to come pick them up.

When Scrap and Bj arrived to pick White Boy and Pooka up, the police were patrolling the area like flies on shit, so they were not able to move from their hiding spot.

Bj told Pooka and White Boy that when they heard some gun shots to come out on Marshfield. He would be right there waiting on them.

Bj dropped Scrap off on Honore, which is 4 blocks from the hiding spot. and went back to the meet up point. Ten minutes later, five shots went off and White Boy and Pooka came running out the gang way and hopped into the back seat of the car. Police cars were flying past doing 50 miles per hour up the street trying to get to where the gun shots went off. After the scene was clear they picked up Scrap and went on about their business.

Tonya sat in the living room watching TV when the news popped on, "This is Susan Monroe from Channel 7 news, live on 50th and Ashland, where 2 men were gunned down while driving south bound on Ashland. Witnesses say that a gray Ford Taurus was chasing this black bronco, as you can see right behind me

137

that crashed into 3 parked cars, firing shots into the truck. Another witness says that the bronco was also firing shots at the Taurus. The shooting started from 48th and Ashland and ended here on 50th and Ashland. We believe that the police gave chase with the Ford Taurus but somehow the killers jumped out the car and fled the scene on foot. I just got some more information in that the Ford Taurus was stolen from the air port on Cicero, so it looks like their intention was to use the stolen car to harm someone. This is 6 deadly shootings in the last 6 weeks. Sources say that there is a war going on with 2 rival gangs. Even though we don't know the motive of the war, we do know that its between Moe-Town, which are the Black Peave Stone Nation and No Love City, which is the Gangster Disciple's. We also hear that the 2 leaders of these 2 gangs are not on the streets. If you have any information about any of the killings that's been going on,, you can call the hot line number at the bottom of your screen or log on the www.channel7.com and go to tips on crimes. I'm Susan Monroe, with you news brief. Thank you for tuning into Channel 7 News."

Tonya was stunned at all the information that the news had. She knew that people talked, but to one another, not the news people and the crazy part about it is that there is no reward even offered for the information. They're just talking for free. She reaches for the phone to contact Bj and let him know what was going on.

Nuke was on the phone trying to get in contact with his lil brother, but no one was picking up the phone. He then tried his wife's phone and still no answer. He then tried his mother's line and got the same results. He also tried his Aunt Dorothy's number but it was restricted. He slams the phone down cause he can't get in touch with anyone.

"Yo, bro, everything alright?" his Latin King buddy asked.

"Yeah, everything's cool. I just couldn't get an answer on any of my lines."

"You need me to make a 3 way for you bro? You know you good people's."

"Naw, it aint' that it's just aint' no one picking up."

"Yo, was that yo peoples on the news??"

"Naw. that was our arch enemies but they mentioned me as being one of the leaders, who is locked up. So that's not good cause before you know it the DEA gone be calling me for a visit about the shit that's goin' on out there and trying to put all types of charges on me."

"Yeah, you right bro. They did my chief like that and when it was time for him to come home, they gave him 10 more murder charges for something he didn't know about."

"I know! That's why I'm trying to get in contact with my lil brother, so he can put a cease to that shit or keep the media's nose out of it."

"Yeah, that's what you have to do bro cause the heat gone fall on you."

"I know right, let me try these numbers again and I'll get back at you in a minute, bro…"

"Alright bro, amour, amour…"

B Real and Monica were laying in the bed after their second

episode of hot sweaty sex. Their really starting to fall for each other, well, at least that's what B Real thinks. He reaches into the top drawer on the night stand next to his bed and pulled out a long black velvet box and a small one too. He handed the long box to her and told her to open it. Her eyes lit up cause she knows the only thing that comes in this type of box is jewelry.

"This for me?"

"Yes, it's for you. Open it."

When she opened it all she saw was the glistening from all the crush diamonds that was laced throughout the chain and charm.

The charm was a cursive J, which supposed to stand for Janet, her alias she's been going by since she met him.

"Thank you boy," she said as she reached for his face and tongued him down.

When she finished kissing him, he handed her a smaller box, which looks like it held arrings ring and told her, "Before you open it I want to tell you how much I feel for you and how much I love you. I know it's been a short time, but you're the first woman that treated me like a real boyfriend and not just for my money, so I'm asking you to be mines forever. Will you marry me, Janet?"

Monica stood there lost for words as her heart was going in two different directions. one was she was feeling loved by someone for the first time in her life and the other one was that this was supposed to only be a job and she was not supposed to fall in love. "Boy, I'm really feeling you and I really care about you, but I'm not saying no, nor am I saying yes. I just want to discuss this with my family and have a little time to think about it."

"Janet, we can go get married in the morning and just leave the country together. I have enough money for both of us to live off of for the 2 life times."

"It's not that boy, cause I feel the same way. I just need some time to make sure I'm making the right choice."

"OK, baby, just make sure you hurry up cause these Chicago streets is moving too fast for me and I don't know how much I can take."

Monica took that as a sign that he's ready to give up but also felt the need to help him. She knows if she crosses Tonya and Bj that her family's life would be in danger and also her life as well. Sooner or later she knows she will have to make a decision and that she doesn't want to do.

"Yo, B, where you at?"

"What the f*ck you mean, where I'm at?"

"You in a crib somewhere? If so, turn to the news. Boo-man and Whino just got hit up on Ashland."

"Dude ____ musta caught them slippin'".

"Aye, Hood, where you at right now?"

"I'm on the block."

"Well, that means you're not where you're supposed to be!"

"What you mean B?"

"If our people's on the news stretched out then I wanna see they people on the news stretched out even worse."

B Real hung up the phone and slammed it on the counter with such force that the clip broke off and flew across the room.

141

'"Baby, you OK? No, I'm tired of this n*gga Bj and his crew. It's bout time for me to put his ass to sleep. Since he really wants to war then let's play ball"

Monica knew she had to say something to let him assume that she' on his side, "Why don't you just hit his pockets. If his money stops flowing then he gets frustrated. Then starts thinking poorly and then you can go in for the kill."

"You know what baby, that sound good. I'm not gone do what he want me to do. He wants to go tit for tat until he catch me slippin. I'm gone hit his money spots then he gone come out and that's when I will have him where I want him at. I'm gone use him as my bunny. I knew it was something about you. That's why I love you girl."

Monica knew she might have put her foot in her own mouth this time, but maybe it can work to her own advantage to get all this shit over with quickly, so she can live a happy life and have some kids and be a wife.

J Hood and his guys sit in 3 different cars outside of one of Bj spots. Traffic was coming and going like they was giving out free food or something. I Hood sat there and watched for an hour, waiting for them to run out of work, so he could run up in there and rob them for all they got. He estimated at least $15,000, as he tried to count al the people that were going in there, but they was coming and going so fast that he lost count a long time ago.

As the line gets down to the last 5 people, J Hood and 6 of his soldiers join the line as if they're trying to shop. They so anxious for the money that they don't recognize the 2 surveillance cameras that watched the line and the door.

Up inside the house, Jake and 2 females were in the kitchen, while one of his guys was at the door jamming the last of the customers. His door security was supposed to be at the door with the pistol, so no one can try to stick the spot up, but instead he's sitting on the couch playing Madden. The person that's upstairs watching the cameras happens to be rolling up a blunt when J Hood gets to the door.

"How many do you want?"

"Can I get five for forty?" J Hood asked.

"You know we don't do plays here clown, so you can take this 4 and get the f*ck on."

J Hood turned around to his man and said, "Yo, let me hold a salt buck till we get back to the crib."

He passed him a $10 bill. When the worker looked down in to the bag to receive one more rock out of it, by the time he looked back up, J Hood had the pistol in his face and he and his guys pushed their way into the crib and shut the door.

Jake sees some movement out he corner of his eye and when he looked clearly he saw his guys being held at gun point. He backs up the back door and left out before he can be noticed. The 2 females looked at him like he was crazy cause he never left them alone to count the money by their selves. Behind them was one of the stick up guys with his gun aimed at them.

"Both of you hoes, put your hands up and don't say a word," was the order.

Both girls did as they were told cause they were scared shitless and didn't want to die over someone else's money.

143

Jake done came to the front of the house and signaled 5 of his guys from down the street to come aid and assist him.

J Hood signaled 2 of his guys to check the upstairs and within minutes they came back down with the guy who was supposed to be watching the spot from the camera at gun point.

Now that they got everyone that's in the house except for Jake, who got away before he can be noticed, at gun point. One guy was in the kitchen stuffing all the money into a duffle bag while 2 of the other guys shake the rest of the house down for drugs and anything else they can find.

Two of the guys who Jake got from down the street, stood on the porch at the door ready for action as they held their guns to their sides and knocked on the door.

J Hood yelled, "We're out. Come back in 20 to 30 minutes."

They knocked on the door again and J Hood said, "Didn't I tell y'all to come back in 20 to 30 minutes?" He peeked out the window and saw that they weren't real customers, but 2 guys holding guns in their hands. He realized that they weren't the police and alerted his guys that there's trouble. Before he can let the guy in the kitchen know to secure the money cause its about to go down, Jake and 3 other guys bum rushed through the back door blazing their guns at the guy who was in the kitchen getting the money.

While J Hood was stilll firing their guns, the front door came crashing in as the 2 guys let off rounds from their guns at J Hood and his guys. J Hood was hit in the shoulder, while the other guy was hit up everywhere and was stretched out on the floor.

As they moved in to finish J Hood off, the 2 guys came

down the stairs firing their guns. One let of his Mac 10 at the guys in the front while the other one fired his P89 Ruger into the kitchen at Jake and his guys. One of the guys in the front room was hit in the back of the head while the other one was hit all in the back.

In the midst of all the shooting, somehow, the 2 females and the other 2 guys that was working the spot was hit by blind bullets.

While the guy was still shooting at Jake in the kitchen, J Hood took that as his chance to flee out the front door. The guy with the P89 Ruger ran out of bullets and tried to reach for one of the guns that was on the floor but was too late as Jake and the other 2 guys ran out of the kitchen in their direction firing numerous shots striking both guys all in their torsos leaving them laid out at the bottom of the stairs.

When Jake made it to the front room, J Hood was speeding away in the car he came in. Jake heard a cry from behind him and turned around to see who it was. It was one of the girls who was helping him count the money asking him not to let her die. He thought about taking her to a hospital but changed his mind when he realized the risk of her tricking, so he added 2 more shots to the one that she already caught to the chest sending her to earn her wings, either upstairs or downstairs.

Jake ran into the kitchen and into the pantry to empty out the safe and grabbed the bag of money from out the dead man's hand and fled out the back door as he heard the police sirens coming up the block.

J Hood went to a hospital all the way on the other side of

town. He almost had 5 different accidents because he kept going in and out of conscious due to all the blood he was losing. When he made it to the hospital, he passed out right on the emergency drive way. A paramedic was trying to pull in, but J Hood's car was blocking the way. The paramedic got out of the ambulance to knock on J's car window. He sees J slumped over in the driver's seat and sees his blood soaked shirt. He reaches in to check for a pulse and rushes him in to the emergency room.

B Real and Monica went to visit Tear Drop today at the hospital. On their way there, Monica was complaining about having headaches and feeling nausea all this morning. She looked at it as a minor problem because it's been coming and going for the last 3 weeks. She made 3 doctor's appointments but every time she was scheduled to be there, she disregarded it cause she was feeling fine on that day,

When they made it to the hospital, her sickness started kicking back in, so she sat down while B Real filled out the paper work so they can visit T Drop. The last time they came to visit him, B Real had put a request in for Monica to be on his visiting list and T Drop's mother had to approve it. He just found out that she was approved to visit.

When he turned around to let her know that she had been approved her saw her leaning as if she was drunk or something. When he started walking towards her asking her if she was alright, she leaned over a lil too much and fell out before he could make it over to her. He called for a nurse to come as he bent down to pick her up.

Two nurses came to assist her, but B Real wouldn't move

out the way as he tried to pick her up off the floor. "Sir, leave her down there, Sir, she need some air," the nurse insisted. as she tried to move him back while the other nurse fanned her. Two more doctors arrived with a stretcher and a neck brace in case she hurt her neck when she fell out, as they put her on the stretcher and wheeled her to one of the exam rooms to begin running some tests.

B Real followed along as if he was a doctor himself. The nurse stopped him at the door and told him that he couldn't enter and that she needs to get some information from about Monica. He started to act a fool, but realized the quicker he gets the nurse out of his face, the quicker he can find out what's wrong with her.

B Real was sitting in the lobby waiting for some news about Monica for half an hour before he decided to go see T Drop while they ran tests on Monica. When he walked into Tear Drop's room, there was a female nurse giving him a bed bath. Then the nurse recognized that he was at the door she spoke and asked him if he can come back in 30 minutes cause she would be through by then.

As he was getting off the elevator on the main floor, he saw the nurse who he had given the information to earlier about Monica, coming out of an office down the hall. He yelled for her attention as he picked up his pace in her direction. "Excuse me, nurse, nurse, can I talk to you a second?"

The nurse stopped so he can catch up with her,

"Have any test results come back on my girlfriend yet?"

"Well, the only thing we found out so far is that she has a

147

mild concussion from when she passed out earlier, but we're going to keep her overnight to run some more tests on her before we release her. You can go home if you like and come pick her up in the morning."

"Can I at least visit her right now?"

"We're not allowed to , but I can try and get you a 5 minute visit, since you're the only guardian that we know of."

"Thank you very much, ma'am!"

"She's in Room 103 and I'll be in there in exactly 5 minutes to end your visit."

"I appreciate that once again mam."

Bj and the guys sat around in the Mason Hall listening to Bj explain what took place at the spot. Bj told Jake that it's a strong possibility that the police is going to be looking for him and that he keep all the cash that he got plus he's going to give him half of a brick of cocaine and send him to Minnesota where his cousin is at and to keep a low profile while he's down there. "I'm gonna call Tony Red and let him know what took place and that he's gonna have o sned someone else to run his blocks and that you're relocating."

"Thanks, bro, aye, Bj I need to spin to my O.G's crib to make sure she's alright and to check on my seeds," Jake said.

"That's not a good idea cause they can probably be at both of their houses right now looking for you. SO just give them a call and once you get finished talking to them, break that phone cause they might have your people's lines tapped and plus when you get to the store, you can get another phone. But don't call your people's NO MORE!" Bj ordered.

"How I'm gone keep in touch with my kids? If you want to stay free then do as I say. You gone have my number at all times, so every 3 weeks, I'm gone send them down there to spend some time with you, but don't let her put anything in her name nor call here to Chicago, while she's down there. Take her phone. Watch her or whatever you have to do, but if you get caught, they gone try to connect you with me and we don't need that and when you call me or anybody don't use your name or whoever you talking to or about on the phones. You got me?"

"Yeah, I got you bro, good looking out!"

"No need bro, you one of mine. This is what I'm supposed to do. You stay here and some one will be here to pick you up and take you to your new destination and remember what I said about them phones."

"I got you bro."

Bj and White Boy were riding and talking when his phone started vibrating. "Hold on for a second, bro. Let me get this call."

"Yeah, what's up Shorty?"

"Oh, so I'm Shorty now?"

"Quit playing so much girl!"

"Oh, I thought you had some female around you that you can't talk around."

"I only f*ck with people who I don't have to hide shit from around me. Ain't no phony snake kickin' it with me."

"Well, I booked you 10 tickets to that fight next week in Las Vegas."

"Girl, you know I don't like the crowd, only for business."

"Oscar do La Hora and Floyd Mayweather gone be fighting and all the ballers and so-called ballers gone be there and I know for sure old girl that you been looking for is going to be there."

"Yeah, you for sure?"

"Sure as good as my p*ssy is."

"Well, I don't think I want to go if that's how sure you is."

"So what you saying n*gga?"

"Girl, I'm just playing, but good looking out. I see I'm gone have to make it up to you some how."

"How about tonight? My back need to be cracked."

"You know we can't do the night thing, but I can be there tomorrow at noon."

"Well don't get too full of wifey's breakfast in the morning that you can't enjoy desert with your mistress."

"Girl, bye. I'll see you at noon."

When Bj got off the phone he turned to White Boy and signaled for him to get off the phone so he can tell him what was new in the makings.

"What's good bro? I had that bitch playing with her p*ssy on the phone, n*gga. She just cumming all over herslf, n*ga. "

"F*ck that hoe, I just got off the phone with Tonya. She got us 10 tickets to the fight next week."

"Yeah, that's what's happening. I already got ten racks on Floyd."

"We gone enjoy the fight but dude gone be there and I'm gone give him his last chance to listen to my offer or its gone be more than lights in Las Vegas. We gone add a whole lot of smoke and fire after we light him and his team up."

"Now, that's even better, plus I want some of that casino money anyway."

"Let Scrap and Pooka know what's up. My other 6 people is gonna be a surprise that I've been waiting to let out the box."

B Real was at the hospital at 8:00 the next morning to pick Monica up. She was scheduled to be released at 9:30, but he thought that he can get there and be able to get her released a lil early. He stopped in the gift shop and bought 2 dozen roses, a card and a teddy bear that had a shirt on that read, 'Get Well, Baby!'. When he walked up to the desk, the lady was on the phone snapping and was acting like he wasn't standing there. He waited a couple more minutes before he started getting impatient. "Miss, I'm here to see a Janet Harris."

She looks on a signing book, while still on the phone, "There's no Janet Harris registered in this hospital, sir."

"Mam, that can't be right. Are you sure she hasn't been signed out already?"

The lady looked again and said, "I'm sorry sir, these kids go me going early this morning. She's still in 103. She's scheduled to check out at 9:30 am."

"Can I go see her now?"

"Sir, it's 8:32 and the visiting hours don't start till 9:00, so I'm not going to be able to let you go up there till 9:00."

"What if I break you off a lil change?" he said as he pulled out a wad of $100 bills.

"I would but my supervisor is doing her rounds and I'm not losing my job sir, but thanks anyway."

151

B Real sat back down in the lobby until he saw the nurse he was talking to yesterday pushing an old man in a wheelchair towards a door that had therapy written over it. HE called out for her and she knew who he was instantly. "Let me take him in here to his therapy coach and I'll be back out to talk to you."

"How you doing sir?"

"I'm fine, just trying to see is my girl alright?"

"She's fine. She should be getting released at 9:30."

"I know. I was trying to sneak in there earlier, but the lady at the desk say that visiting hours don't start till 9:00 and that she would have let me up but her supervisor is doing her rounds."

"Yeah, that's right, but if you want me to take that to her room, I will."

"IT's cool. I wanted to surprise her, but I'll just wait till she comes down."

"Alright then, make sure you take care of her and keep her from stressing a lot, especially now since she's..." The nurse caught herself before she let any more information out her mouth. She's not supposed to tell a patient's business unless they're not able to tell it themselves.

"What were you about to say? Since she's what?"

"I'm sorry sir. I was just running my mouth a li too much. I'm sure she will talk to you about everything. I've got to get back to my work before I get chewed out by my boss this morning."

The nurse rushed away and B Real looked at her like she was crazy, but was stilll trying to figure out what she was goin to say before she caught herself. So he went back to the lobby and sat and waited for Monica to be released.

B Real was sitting in the lobby lost in this own thought until he realized that he hasn't heard from J Hood since yesterday at noon. So he called his cell phone and it went right to the voice mail. He tried again and again and again. Always the same thing. He then tried calling one of the guys who be around him a lot and stilll came up short. He then decided that he would take a ride through the hood once Monica was released.

B Real had fell asleep in the chair watching for Monica to be released. She tip toed over to the chair where he was sleeping at after she finished signing out and getting her prescriptions and kissed him on the lips. He jumped up in a fighting stand until he realized who it was.

"Girl, you almost got knocked out doing that! You know not to mess with a man when he's asleep and tired at that for me to fall asleep in a chair. Shit I thought I was at home for a minute."

"Boy, please, I wish you would think about hitting me with your crazy self. You'll be going past a hospital right to somebody's morgue."

"Is that a threat girl?"

"Naw, boo a promise."

"And you talking about I'm crazy. Girl, let's get up out of here before I sign you into a crazy room. I know they got one here as big as this other f*cker is."

"You gone sign right in with me too. They gone call us the crazy couple."

The nurse behind the desk started laughing her head off as she sat there listening to the 2 of them go at it in a funny way.

153

On the ride home, B Real and Monica made small talk here and there and Monica sensed something was on his mind and Monica sensed something and thought it was him starting to stress out about all the shit that's been going on. She looked over at him and rubbed his shoulder as she asked if everything was alright. He turned the radio all the way down and said, "Bay, I want to ask you a questions and please don't lie to me. Just tell me the true."

Monica had a look on her face as she realized she's been caught empty handed with her pants down. She doesn't know if she should swing first or just jump out the car while it is stilll running. "The doctor was telling me the reason you passed our was because you was under a lot of stress."

Monica let the air out of her chest as she realized that it wasn't what she thought he was going to ask her and now knew that soon – before it's too late – she's going to have to make a decision on which way she wants to go and who she's going to ride with.

"The doctor was about to let something slip out her mouth, but she caught herself and said that she's not allowed to tell the patient's business and she's sure that you would share it with me. What was she talking about?"

Monica paused for a second before saying, "They told me that my blood pressure was high and that I might be catching diabetes."

B Real sensed that she was lying, but choose to let it go for now, while praying she didn't have any type of STD or something.

The rest of the ride home, Monica was in her own thoughts as well as B Real. "You, you hungry?" she asked.

"Yeah, what do you have a taste for? It's your call. I know that hospital food was horrible."

"Who you telling? Let's go to Gramm's Kitchen on 79th and have some breakfast. I got a taste for some of their chopped steak omelet with extra extra cheese."

"Yeah, I like their blueberry pancakes, plus they be thin and not that thick shit like everybody else."

The restaurant was crowded, like always, but they were stilll able to get a seat. They made their order and sat waiting for about 20 minutes before they were served their food. B Real dived straight in, not caring how hot it was or nothing. On the other hand, Monica took her time putting salt and pepper on it and chopping it up so that she wouldn't choke off the big pieces of meal that was in there.

"Bay, you already have high blood pressure, so you better take it easy on that salt, you know.

"I'm just putting a little bit on there for the taste."

Monica took a fork full of her food and the quicker she swallowed it, the faster she threw it up into a napkin. B Real pushed the rest of his food to the side cause his appetite had just been spoiled. "Bay, you alright over there?"

"Yeah, I don't know why my stomach won't let me eat this, probably cause of my system being clean or maybe I am a diabetic already. I'm just going to try and eat this raisin bread and see if it will hold."

She tried the raisin bread and it stayed down, but when she tried the omelet agin, the same thing happened. "Well, I'm going call my doctor and see what it is that I can and can't eat."

B Real and Monica got up, paid for the food and headed to his house.

Bj, the guys and Tonya and her girls all took a trip out to Michigan City mall to find something to wear to the fight tomorrow. Bj had met with Mystery Co-C0 and three more of his special affect team girls and let them know what would take place at the fight if his enemy don't agree to meet on his terms and that this is the last offer he's sending.

Bj pulled up to the front entrance of the arena in a silver Bentley SLC coupe while White Boy followed behind him in a Lexus Cope and Scrap and Pooka riding in a Cadillac CLR. Everyone watches the 3 silver bullets come to a halut. Bj hops out wearing a black Armani suit with silver stripes and a silver and black 3 quarter length chinchilla coat. He handed the valet a folded up $100 bill as his guys hopped in their car to go park it.

White followed with the same kind of suit and chinchilla, except his was navy blue and silver. Scrap had on royal blue and silver and Pooka had on white and dark silver. They all walked in together as the flashes went uncontrollable from the onlookers cameras.

The guys mingled around with all typed of top notch stars as well as rappers and sports players. After all the phony chit chatting, they headed to their seats as the girls waited for them. When Bj noticed Tonya he was amazed by her new look. Not just because of her beauty, but because he know that B Real wouldn't be able to recognize her as the one from the party.

B Real walked in with a fine ass chick on his arm. She was giving Tonya a run for her money. They both had on black and gray. B Real had on a short black mink and she had on a short gray mink. As they got closer, he noticed that the chick he had with him was Monica and instantly he had a bulge in his pants that went down as he thought about his enemy sticking his cock in her. B Real finally glanced over in Bj's direction and both nodded their heads at each other as they intend on watching a good fight tonight.

The first, second and third rounds were full of love taps as both fighters try to figure out each other's weakness. Bj and B Real also had their stare down with each other and the thing that broke their stares was when one of the fighters got a good hit in and the crowd went wild.

Bj leaned over and whispered something in Tonya's ear before the both of them got up from their seats. Bj's guys got up to follow, but he waved them off and headed over towards B Real and his 15 to 20 soldiers that he had with him.

Once Bj made it over there B Real and his date stood up, as they all sized each others appearance up and down, all of B Real's guys stood up but was quickly told to sit back down. B Real's seat was at the end of the row, so they was not in no one's way of them not being able to see the fight.

B Real spoke first in a cocky way, "I see we finally meet again."

"Well, I tried to make it earlier this month in a comfort zone that was best for the both of us, but things kind of got out of

157

hand."

"You know how it is when us black folks get liquor in our system. It's hard to talk on a man to man level."

"Well, speak for yourself cause I'm a light drinker, so I can always be a good thinker."

"What brings you over here to my side of the arena?"

"I came over here to try once again to set up a meeting for the both of us to discuss our differences and move on to a better crime free life."

"well, let's meet on my terms and my term only or we can end this conversation now and may the best man win."

"I thought maybe it was the liquor the last time, but now I see you like to abuse your power."

"Maybe that's the case then."

"We'll see both of us has power and there's only two ways that being in power goes. One is that we come to a neutral agreement , so that the both of us can enjoy our power or two, we go by the saying that said, 'This town ain't big enough for the both of us' and like you say, 'May the best man win'".

"See that's what I like about you – you look at things both ways. The only problem is you fail to realize is that I don't share things and I'm a pace setter, not a negotiator."

Bj looks at him for a second then says, "I see, may the best man win and as you can see, I've been doing the winning. Well, enjoy your fight night now cause I got a surprise for you when you least expect it." Bj walked away and thought to himself, that's if he makes it out of Vegas.

Tonya and Monica locked eyes and Tonya couldn't tell for

sure if Monica was stilll on their side and plus she hasn't talked to Monica in 3 or 4 days. She made a mental note in her head to meet with her and see what's what cause she brung her in according to Bj. She's going to have to be the one to take her out if she's flipped sides.

The flight went to the 11th round and just as the clock hits 35 seconds Floyd goes in for the kill with 2 left jabs, a right hook which Oscar ducks, but couldn't move away from the left upper cut that sent him to the pavement for a ten count.

As everyone started leaving the arena, Bj and his people went straight to their rides while B Real and his entourage stayed in the lobby show boating with all the other celebrities as if they were stars.

Mystery and her crew came strutting through the lobby and everyone's attention was on them including the females. They had on their tight fitting versa chi dresses looking like 5 angels from heaven.

Usher, Jahem and a few more other stars shot their shots but came up short and when they approached B Real and his crew, the stars wondered who they were that they were able to pull the girls in their direction when every   so call important celeb got shot down.

When Monica seen Mystery she knew it was trouble but didn't know what to do. She was feeling the urge to let B Real know who the girls were and what they were about until she seen Tonya facing her before going into the ladies room, she stood at the door signaling Monica to come join her. She hesitated but turned to B Real to let him know that she was going to the ladies

159

room. B Real took that as a good chance to shoot his shot at the leader of the crew, which was Mystery.

When Monica made it into the ladies room, Tonya was a the sink fixing her makeup. Monica joined her and said, "What's up, T?", as if they done been in touch with each other for the last week.

"That's what I'm trying to find out. I haven't heard from you in the last 4 or 5 days, so I was hoping that you ain't fall for that clown and switching sides on us."

"Why would you think that Tonya?"

"Cause its like everywhere he's at you're at."

"That's because I had to act as if we are really as one in order for him to trust me. He even got it where I'm on the list to see T Drop anytime I want. Ain't that what my job is? Ain't I suppose to try and get his family whereabouts, so don't you disrespect me as being a trader cause I would never disrespect you like that."

"Nick, I wasn't saying it like that. I was just making sure we're stilll on the right page."

"T, you're like a sister to me. You the only sister I got right now and trust with my life. Don't make me think other."

Tonya wanted to snap on her, but knew she had to hold her tongue in order to get the job done but later on she would pay for her mouth.

Both girls had embraced each other for what seems like a life time in the ladies room before exiting. Monica came out first and felt a little heartbroken as she watched B Real flirt with Mystery. He saw her coming and acted as if they was talking as a

160

whole group. Monica walked up and locked arms with B Real as if she was claiming her throne, but winked at Mystery to let her know that she's aware of what's going on. Mystery backed up and signaled for her girls to follow suit.

Tonya calls Bj and let him know that she had the talk with Monica and that she's still on the team. In the middle of their conversation, his other line clicks. He looks at the caller ID and sees that it's Mystery and tells Tonya that he will call her back after he gets off the other line.

"What's up Ree?"

"Everything's going good on my end. Me and the ladies is hanging out with some friends at 10:00 tonight at the Hilton Hotel on the 22nd floor. I know you don't like being around n*ggas that you don't know, but you would want to be there."

"Naw, I'm going to take a rain check on that one. I trust you to behave yourself and clean up after yourself."

"Ok, well, I'll call you in the morning and maybe we can make it our business to see each other."

"That will be lovely."

"I'll be looking forward to seeing you and one more thing,…"

"What' that Ree?"

"You looked edible tonight and I wasn't able to let you know, so now I'm telling you."

"Thanks and you was beautiful yourself."

"Wait till you see me in the morning then."

"I can't wait."

Bj sat in his hotel room waiting to receive the call from Mystery. He heard a tap on his room door and wondered who could it be. He looked through the peep hole and saw that it was Tonya, wearing her pink house coat. When he opened the door, she sashayed in like the badest bitch in the world. Before Bj can even shut the door, she dropped her house coat to reveal that she had on what she came in to this world with and that was nothing. Bj attacked her in the most sexiest way. They went at it to the wee hours of the morning.

Bj woke up from the beeping sound of his cell phone, which lets him know that he has some voice mails. He reached and grabbed the phone to listen to his messages.

Monica sat in her and B Real's hotel room with all types of thoughts going through her head. One was the conversation that her and Tonya had earlier and the other one is what could be happening to her supposed to be enemy/baby daddy.

She reached for her phone to call B Real but set it back down cause she felt that she couldn't trade on her friend, but then she grabbed it again as she realized the her son or daughter is going to need their father if she decides to keep it.

The first 2 times she called his phone she got no answer. She tried again 10 minutes later and he answered. She had her story already made up as if she's been practicing for year.s

"Bay, I need you to come to the room right now. I've been blacking out and I don't have my pills. I need you to stop downstairs and get me some ibuprofen and then you can go back outside."

"Alright, I'll be there in 10 minutes."

Twenty minutes passed and Monica had to wonder if he had made it out or not, so she called him again. It went straight to his voice mail. She tried a few more times and the same thing happened. She knew then that it was over and instantly felt empty.

When B Real got off the phone, he went back to the party. When he entered the adjoining room, all he saw were tits and asses everywhere. Mystery was doing this trick with a Moet bottle, where she had it moving it and out of her vagina without touching it.

Mystery and the girls had some chains and bracelets on that was clear and were made to glow in the dark. "Fellas we're going to turn this party up a notch. We going to turn the lights off and when you see some lights glow then you know that' one of us waiting to be pleased, "Monica announced.

A knock at the door and 10 of Mystery's friends joined the party with just thongs and bras on. The lights went out and the party got cracking. B Real slipped out the door so that he can take Monica her pills and get back to the party.

B Real made it to his room and Moica was sitting on the couch with a mug on her face as if she was mad at the world.

"What's wrong with you girl?"

"I could be laying here dead or something, as long as you took."

"It ain't been nothing more than 20 minutes since I talked to you."

"More like 30 minutes when you told me 10!"

"Here is your pills you ask for. DO yo need anything else?"

163

"Do you have to go back outside? I want you to stay with me."

"Bay, me and the fellas is bout to hit the Empress to see if we can win a million or more," B Real said with a serious face.

She knew he was lying but she figured the longer she can keep him there, she can save his life. "You have enough money already."

"There's never enough money, if I can go out and win ten million tonight then I can give you two million tomorrow."

"I don't want to be rich. I need to be loved!"

"I do love you and show you love, don't I?"

"Yeah, I just want you to stay with me tonight."

"Bay, just give me 3 hours and I promise that we can stay in all tomorrow and make love."

Monica went at it with the questions for about 15 to 20 minutes until he finally got her to give in and let him go. The moment he left she prayed that she kept him long enough to save his life for the moment, but sooner or later it's not going to be anything she can do, unless she flips sides.

B Real walked back into the hotel room with his mind on Mystery and how he's going to try and break her back. As he walked through the first room heading toward to connecting room, he can hear the music playing which lets him know that it's stilll crackin. He opens the door hoping to see the glow in the dark. Lights are off all over the place, but the room was pitch black. Five steps in to the room he stumbles over what feel like a body laying on the floor. He steps over it as he figures that the

164

girls and guys was getting it on.

As he walks further into the room, he comes across another body, but this time he tripped and fell. He landed in something wet and got mad. He jumped up and turned on the lights. As soon as the lights came on he looked as if he'd seen a ghost. All of his men was sprawled out everywhere. Some was bleeding from their necks, mouth and faces. He looked to his right and saw that one of his guys was laying flat on his stomach, but his head was facing straight up to the ceiling like someone had twisted his neck all the way around. Out of the corner of his eye, he saw some movement and turned in that direction to see what it was. One of his guys was stilll alive but for some reason he couldn't talk or move his body.

B Real went over to him trying to help him up but he felt like dead weight. He asked him some questions, but all he did was blink his eyes as tears came down. B Real could feel his pain, but looked at him as a bitch ass n*gga for crying. He didn't want to leave him there with the rest of them but figured he would probably open his mouth to the police, so he took the pillow off the couch and suffocated him. He then went in to the washroom and grabbed a dry towel and some disinfectant and went around both rooms wiping things off that can lead a trace back to him, as he was wiping off the table in the first room, there was a note on the table that was signed by Mystery that read, "That's twice that you done escaped death. The best thing to do is throw the towel in cause as sure as my name Mystery, I promise you that the third time you will be history."

B Real grabbed the note and set it in the ashtray and lit a

165

match to it and watched it burn as he knew now that this was one of Bj's stunts and how he escaped death.

He made it to his room in 5 minutes and he and Monica packed and got on the first plane back home. The whole ride home they only made small talk and not about what happened at the hotel. On the other hand, Monica know but was glad that he escaped.

Bj woke up early and left before Tonya got up. As he was walking towards Mystery's room, he dialed her number. She answered her phone on the first ring.

"Rise and shine or I can turn back around."

"The door is open sweetie."

Bj walked into the room with nothing but sex on his mind. The smell of peaches and cream filled his nostrils. Mystery yelled from the washroom, "I'll be out in a minute, unless you want to come join me."

Bj jumped on the offer and got undressed in no time and headed to the washroom.

As he entered, Mystery she had her back turned towards the door, so he can see how big her ass is. His cock got hard instantly as he watched the soap suds run down the crack of her ass. She moved to the side, so he can join her. The little steps that she took has her ass shaking out of control.

He grabbed the soapy sponge and started at her upper shoulder and made it back down to her waist. He continued on down as he washed her butt cheeks and thighs. Mystery spread her legs so he can have easy way to her cave, as he washed her

166

p*ssy he tried to turn her around so he can do her front as well but she stopped him and told him, "You got to spread the cheeks and get all up in there boo. Don't be scared. I do it twice a day, sometimes three."

Bj spread her ass cheeks and washed all in the crack of her ass and her p*ssy some more as well. Mystery started moaning and moving with the rhythm of his hand, as he came back down to her p*ssy.. He came across her ass hole with his thumb and in the same timing, she was pushing up on his hand and his thumb went into her ass hole. She let out a moan even louder as if she was feeling it. Bj dropped the sponge and planted his penis inside her p*ssy from the back, as he took slow short strokes.

He was sticking his thumb in and out of her ass. Mystery leaned over farther until she had her hand on the base of the tub and started throwing her ass at him, so that he can put all of him inside of her. He held her soft cheeks so that he cold be in control as he continued to tease her with the small strokes. He wanted to just demolish her but he knew if he did she wouldn't enjoy it cause of the three rounds that him and Tonya had last night.

He pulled out and bent down to grab the sponge to wipe himself off. Mystery grabbed the sponge out of this hand and reached for his penis at the same time. After wiping it off a few times, she puts some fresh, clean water on it before swallowing him whole. She took all of him in without exercising her jaws for the ride. Bj almost came in her throat instantly as he felt the back of her throat and the vibrating she was doing from humming.

She felt him jerk and knew it was time for breakfast in a few

167

seconds. She went up and down as she jagged him off to feed herself. As soon as she tasted the first drop, she let him all the way in her throat as she jiggled his balls to make sure she got the full load. She kept him in her mouth until she knew it wasn't dripping no more. She'd rather drink it all than to let a man shoot any of it inside her. She doesn't believe in abortion and is not ready for any kids so she specializes in knowing when a male is about to cum.

Mystery and Bj washed each other up some more then took the action to the bedroom.

As soon as Bj got in foot range of the master bed, Mystery took over by pushing him on to the bed and jumping on top of him. Bj was rock hard so she had no problem as she sat down on him and went for the ride of a lifetime. Bj went crazy as she took control. She was moving up and down on him so fast without letting him slip out of her. After 10 minutes of putting her work in Bj flipped her over cause he knew he would be busting off any minute now. He positioned himself in between her legs as she laid on her side with one leg up. As soon as he slid in her, he got to pumping away, like there was no tomorrow. He felt himself ready to explode and kept pumping cause it felt good. Mystery also felt his head swell up and knew it was time. He jerked and tried to keep pumping but she pushed him off and pulled herself from his grip and went for a drink as he shot half of it in her face as she caught the rest. She is so use to the taste of um that she wiped the nut that was running down her face with her middle finger and licked it off her finger as if it was some cake frosting.

Bj went to take him a quick shower and returned back to the

168

room where Mystery was stilll laying in the bed trying to recuperate.

"So how did your job turn out last night?"

"Well, let's just say, I took everyone out except for my direct target."

"What do you mean by that?" Bj asked as he realizes that the fight isn't over.

"I know you might not believe me, but I think your girl, Monica is playing both sides of the field."

"I don't think so, but why do you think that and what does that have to do with him getting away?"

"See we was at the room getting our party on and just when everyone was tipsy and our plan was bout to be into effect, I'm giving B Real a lap dance and his phone starts ringing. I see her name pop up on the screen, so he told me to give him a second as he got up to talk on his phone. Five minutes later, he comes back to the party and pulls me to the side, as he starts licking on my nipples, the rest of my crew show up so that all the guys can be accommodated. Once everyone had a partner I signaled for the lights to be cut off. All the girls had on glow in the dark chains and bracelets, so I would know where they were at once the lights went out. As soon as the lights went out, his phone lights up, as if he has an incoming call and I see the light fade off to the door. Five minutes had past and he didn't return so we took everyone else in the party out and left."

"So you saying that Monica kept calling him and probably signaled for him to leave?"

"She had to cause I was informed that she knew what was up and

169

was told to fall back but if that was so then why would she be calling him?"

"That's a good questions and I'm going to find out and she better hope she's not cause her and her family going to be buried alive."

Bj reached into his pocket to retrieve the money he brought with him to pay Mystery and tossed it to her. She caught it and tossed it back to him. Your sex was a good enough pay for me and I hope we can continue it on a regular."

"Well, I'm getting married in a few months, so I don't know what to say."

Mystery didn't like the sound of them words, "Well I always get what I want, so I'm not worried. Plus that's too much time for me. Don't be surprised to see me in that dress next to you."

"Girl, I don't think so. I love my boo."

"Yeah, Okay sweetie. Be careful what you love, cause lust always wins."

Bj put the money back in his pocket and left thinking about B Real getting away and if Monica was playing both sides or what or can he trust Mystery.

Bj and his crew arrived at Midway airport late that night. Everyone was tired so they went their separate ways to get them some rest and start the next day fresh. Tonya invited Bj over for the rest of the night, but he declined the offer. He wanted to get peace of mind alone in his own palace, plus he could use the sleep cause he hadn't had much since he been home from jail.

Bj walked into his home and sat on the couch in the mood to

catch a little sports center before he called it a night. As he reached for the remote on the table he noticed the light on the phone blinking. He pushed the button to listen to his messages. All of them was from his finance, except for the last one which was his mother letting him know that they're having a wonderful time. He turned the TV on and it was already on the CNN news channel that had breaking news going across the screen. He listened as they talked about the episode that took place in Las Vegas. After he was some what satisfied that they had no evidence on the killers, he flipped to the sports channel to catch the scores and highlights before falling asleep on the couch.

Bj pulled up to Harold's chicken joint on 56th and Ashland, as soon as he got out the car and closed his door a dark blue Astro van pulled up, the side door flew open exposing a masked man wih a Mac 10 pistol pointed in his face. "Bitch don't move or I'll blow your muther f*cking brains out," was the order.

Bj didn't know what to do as he was caught off guard. His mind was telling him to run but his heart was telling him to do as he was told.

The guy in the passenger seat jumped out and forced him into the van. Bj gave a little struggle until he was hit in the back of the head with the butt of a gun and thrown into the van. The guy that was in passenger seat jumped into Bj's car and followed the van to a warehouse where B Real was waiting for them.

When Bj woke up from the cold water that was splashed in his face, he realized that he couldn't move because he was duct taped to a chair in a dark room with one big ass overhead light. When he saw who was standing in front of him he knew then

171

that this would be his final resting spot.

"IF it ain't the infamous Bj! My, my, my. what a surprise. I bet you didn't think you would ever end up in this position, huh? What you say, oh, my bad. You can't talk with that tape around your mouth. I would take it off, but I'm not in the mood to listen. Tonight I will be doing all the talking and the action, so sit back and enjoy the pain."

B Real put on some gloves that had patches of sand made where the knuckles are. He walked up to Bj and hit him with a right jab that broke his nose instantly. He then threw a left jab that knocked both his top and bottom front teeth out.

Bj was bleeding like a hog from his nose and his mouth. After B Real got tired of boxing practice, he took a 10 minute cigarette break while talking shit to Bj.

Bj heard every word that was being said to him but couldn't see a thing cause his eyes were swollen shut from the punches he had taken. B Real knocked him out at least 15 times and every time he knocked him out, he woke him up with a power blow.

Bj was in so much pain but couldn't show any weakness. He done been in the same place as B Real so many times and didn't like no coward begging for their life so he wouldn't dare beg for his.

B Real knew that Bj believed in Allah as his God, so he wanted to play a game with him. He pulled out a 5 shot 38 revolver and pointed it at Bj's right arm. "I wish you can see this but your windows are shut. I'm going to talk and act it out. One day while I was in jail this Muslim brother used to go around the deck trying to convince everybody to become a Muslim. He turned the first 3 people and was teaching them how to call prayer. The next 6 people tried it, but found it to be complicated so they fell back. You following me Bj or you falling asleep on me?" B Real got up and slapped Bj to make sure he was stilll listening. When he saw Bj try to shake the blow off, he knew he was stilll woke.

"So when I ask the Muslim cat why do they call God Allah? He told me that it stands for God in physical form. I didn't understand at first, until he was like name a part on your body that start with 'a'. As soon as I said 'arm' he punched me." so B Real shot Bj in the right arm. A muffle came from Bj's mouth, but he was stilll tried playing the tough man roll.

As B Real spelled out the word he did as the Muslim had done to him, but instead of punching, he shot Bj in the spots. When he made it to the 'H' he paused and talked mega shit before shooting Bj in the forehead. Bj flipped over in the chair and landed on his back. His chest was stilll moving up and down as he took his last breath thinking about his past. As soon as his breathing stopped everything was quiet.

Bj woke up in a cold sweat, breathing hard as he realized he was having a bad dream and that he wasn't dead. He got up off the couch stilll a little f*cked up from the dream he had just had and went to take him a hot shower and clear his head.

On the other side of town, B Real got up bright and early to form his team for an all out war against Bj and his crew. Lately, Bj been scoring real good. B Real lost a lot of guys at the club and now at the fight and he hasn't heard from J Hood in almost 2 weeks, since he was supposed to rob one of Bj's spots.

173

Bj was on his way to the head, until he got a call from Tiffany asking him was he going to be in court for Nuke today. He told her yeah, when really he forgot that today was his court date. He then made a detour right to the county jail.

When he made it in the court room, the judge was just calling Nuke's name. He was glad that he didn't have to sit in the court room long and was also glad he didn't miss it cause he would have never heard the last from his brother.

"Sir, is you Demarcus Barker?" the judge asked.

"Yes, sir, your honor."

:And you are his attorney, right?"

"Your honor, Mr. Belgin is running late, but I'm his assistant, Mr. Willbly."

"What are you doing today, sir?"

"We are here for a bond sir. My client has a pregnant wife at home who needs him plus he's a working man sir. I have signed documents her from the president of Zippy's Steel and Welding Company showing that my client is a working man and the provider for his household, sir."

"OBjection your honor," the state's attorney yelled out. "This man is a gang leader and also a drug lord."

"Your honor, the state doesn't have any evidence to prove these accusations."

The judge looked at the state's attorney and asked her, "Do you have anything to prove what you're saying?"

"Not at this time your honor, but if you give me a 2 weeks continuance I will have all the facts.""

"Your honor, my client has been locked up for close to 3 months now. If you won't give him a bond, can you at least put him on home monitoring, so he can be at home with his pregnant wife?"

"Your honor, this man was out on bond for an attempt on a police officer and fleeing the scene and now he's back on a possession of an unregistered firearm. He's a flight risk, your honor. I ask that he be held with a bond hold till trial," the state's attorney pleaded.

The judge was looking over some papers before stating, "I'm not going to put a hold on his bond just yet."

Nuke had a surprised look on his face as he figured he's about to get a bond, until the judge finished talking,

"Nor am I going to give him a bond. I am going to give the state a 2 week continuance to prove their motive on why this man shouldn't have a bond and you better have something in black and white," the judge admonished the state's attorney.

Before Nuke left out the court room, he turned around to face his little brother and made a sign with his hand to let Bj know that he's going to call him, so make sure he answers the phone.

In the back bullpen Nuke was going hard on his attorney's assistant telling him to tell his broyer, "I pay him too much mother f*cking money for him to be missing court dates. Tell him I want to see his ass today or he can get ready to write me a check and I can get someone else to represent me who deserves my money and I mean he better be to see me today."

"Alright, Mr, Barker. I will let him know as soon as I can

make a phone call, just don't stress yourself out."

"And one more thing, thanks for the good job you did today. We almost had him to give me a bond. I wish you was able to get this money, but I know you can't cross him."

"You just take care of yourself and I'm going to deliver your message."

B Real had formed him a new army and was finishing his last statement to the crew about his plan for tonight. As soon as he departed from everyone, his phone started ringing. He looked at the caller ID and saw it was J Hood. He answered it with a lot of aggression in his voice. "Where the f*ck you been Hood? Don't tell me you on some grimey shit n*gga or I'm gone do you in real bad, bro."

"Hold on, Real! I've been in the…"

B Real jumps in before he can even finish the statement with, "Where the f*ck you at right now? Meet me at Fat Albert's in 20 minutes and don't have me waiting long either." B Real hung up the phone before he could respond.

J Hood walked in Fat Albert's restaurant not knowing what to expect to go down because he knew from the tone in his boss's voice that this won't be a good meeting.

One of the guys holding the door open that leads to the back of the restaurant. As he was walking past that guy, he tried to give some daps but the guy just looked at his hand like it was poisonous. Right then and there, he decided to turn back around and never return, but he kept on through cause he knew he didn't have anything to hide.

When he entered the back room, there was a chair sitting in

the middle of the room with 2 guys standing on both side of it. He saw his boss standing off to the side talking on his cell phone and as soon as they made eye contact, he hung up the phone and motioned for J Hood to sit down in the chair.

Hood's right arm was in a sling form the shot he took to the shoulder at the shoot out at one of Bj's spots. "What's all the tension for Real?" Hood asked.

"Why don't you tell me. I haven't heard from you in 2 weeks. The last time I saw you - you was supposed to be robbing Bj's spot and I know he had a lot of cake in there cause that's one of his main spots. So where the drugs and the money at?" B Real quizzed.

"I've been in t hospital since that day. We went in the spot but things got ugly. We had a shoot out throughout the house, but they ended up winning. Everybody else was killed and I was hit in the shoulder. I was able to get out the house before they killed me and drive myself to the hospital. They had me in ICU cause I lost a lot of blood. I just got out 3 days ago."

"Why didn't you call me since then and I know you got away with some drugs and money," B Real countered.

"I swear I didn't get a chance to get nothing. Mike had the bag full of money in the kitchen before he was shot up from who ever came in through the back door."

"For some reason, I don't believe you, but I'm going to take your word."

"I swear Real, I wouldn't cross you. You been good to me. You all I got bro."

"I don't care how f*cked up your arm is, but we got a job to

177

do tonight so get prepared."

B Real and his guys was leaving out the restaurant when he saw a thick ass broad putting some food in the passenger side of the car. He approached her from behind. "Do you need some help with that baby girl?" When the girl turned around he couldn't believe who it was. Instantly he signaled for his guys to grab her and take her back in to the restaurant. She tried to give a fight, but the guys were too strong for her.

Once they made it back in the back room, she was tied up to the same chair that J Hood thought he was just about to loose his own life in not 10 minutes before.

"Well, well, well, what a surprise! I know you would have never thought you would get caught with your panties down, huh?"

"You lucky, I had my panties down or you would be laid out front with a white line around you!"

"I see you stilll tough even though you about to loose your life."

She calmed down as she realized that her mouth was digging her deeper.

"What is it you want? I got paper, drugs, hoes. What ever you want."

"See I got all of that you just named and you know damn well. That's not what I want, your bitch ass man is who I want. Now I wonder if he would trade himself for you?"

"You might as well gone do what you want to do to me cause I ain't no trick bitch who would give up my guy for my life. Everything that's been going on, I had parts in it, so I accept what's coming to me."

"I like a bitch like you. It's hard to find one these days."

"I'm not your bitch, so watch your mother f*cking mouth!"

"You what ever, I call you bitch, hoe, slut. I run this shit!"

"You don't run shit but your mouth!"

B Real hauled off and slapped slob out of her mouth. Blood started running down the corner of her mouth.

"You feel good now that you put your hands on a lady? Do it again, maybe you would get a nut off cause I just came all over myself."

"Bitch you think this a game, huh?" he points to J Hood and orders, "Strip that bitch clothes off.. I'm bout to show her how to get a nut."

J Hood started doing as he was told. As soon as he got her pants down to her knees her phone started ringing.

"Hand me that bitch phone."

"I told you already, I'm not your bitch!"

"Put something in that bitch mouth cause I'm tired of hearing her right now."

B Real looked at the caller ID and saw that it was a female named Monica and then pressed end. He then went into her phone book to see if she had BK's number stored. When he came across Bj's number, he pressed send to make the call.

Bj answered on the second ring. "What's up shorty?"

"What's up Mr. Bj?" B Real asked.

"Who the f*ck is this playing on my phone?"

"Oh, you don't recognize my voice by now? This is your worst nightmare!"

Bj then picked up on his voice. "If you lay one finger on her, I swear…"

"Be cool, homie. She's in good hands. I would let you talk to her, but she got dick stuck in her mouth. I mean a sock in her mouth. Ha, ha, ha…"

"What do you want?"

"Let's see. What is this bitch worth?"

She started saying something but the sock was stopping the noise, so all you could hear was mumbles.

He put the phone on speaker and then snatched the sock from her mouth and instantly she went on the rampage.

"I got your bitch as soon as I get a chance. Bj f*ck this n*gga let him do what he got to do to me."

"Where you find this hoe at cause I need one like her?"

She tried to go at it again, but he stuffed the sock back in her mouth.

"Now let me see, what I want for her…"

Bj cut him off, "Well as you can see kill that bitch. She wants to die." then the phone went dead.

B Real tried to call him back but he didn't answer. So he tried a few more times, stilll no answer. He then got mad and walked over to her. He sees a smile on her face. "So you think shit's funny, huh?"

He starts to unbutton his pants. "Let's see you laugh now as me and my guys run trains on you till your p*ssy starts bleeding like a water fountain."

180

J Hood and 3 other guys took her from the chair and tied her arms to both rails of the bed. B Real positioned himself in between her legs and was shocked that she didn't' resist. "I see you want this just as much as I want it, huh?"

she shook her head up and down agreeing with what he said.

He entered her with a slow stroke as if he's in the mood to make love. He then takes the sock out of her mouth to see if she's going to moan or talk shit.

"That's all you get n*gga. You better beat this p*ssy up like it's yours."

B Real then started pounding away like a mad man. She kept talking shit trying to assassinate his character. but it got him more excited. Ten minutes later, he jerked as he felt himself bout to explode. He pulled out and shot his semen all over her stomach.

"That's all you got, 10 minutes? Who's next cause this p*ssy is just getting wet."

J Hood was the first one to get his shot next. As soon as he entered her she started going crazy as if he was too big for her. "Oh shit daddy, yeah, just like that tear this p*ssy up, ooh, shit yeah." She put on a show as J Hood thought he was "The Man".

"This dick better than your boss. You should be the boss."

That struck a nerve with B Real, as he stuck the sock back in her mouth forcing it almost down her throat cutting her wind off. She gagged a few time, as she started turning purple in the face. He then pulled out some so she could breathe out her nose.

The phone started ringing and B Real seen it was Bj again. "So I see you changed your mind, huh? I must say one thing

181

though, she got some good ass p*ssy man."

""I must agree with you, but I got someone who I'm about to test out as well and from the looks of it her stomach is getting big like she's pregnant. You want to speak to her?"

B Real felt like he was stabbed in the chest, as he hoped that it ain't his Janet.

"Hello, hello, you stilll there? Put her on the phone!"

B Real motioned for J Hood to stop what he was doing,but he kept going trying to get his nut off. B Real then yelled, "Muther f*cker didn't I tell you to stop?"

J Hood then pulled out and pulled his pants up.

"Bay, please come and get me. He talking about killing our child."

"What child? You never told me about no baby."

"When the nurse caught herself at the hospital that's what she was bout to tell you but I told her not to cause I was going to tell you myself."

"That's enough of the baby mama and baby daddy shit, you got 72 hours for Shorty to be out of your hands and back into mine or you can have one more under your belt, while I add 2 under mine, " Bj ordered.

"It don't take 72 hours. Let's pick a meeting spot that's good for both of us and swap it out."

"Just keep the phone close and wait for my call But in the mean time, I got to get me a shot of this p*ssy. They say pregnant p*ssy is the best p*ssy and I'm bout to find out."

The phone went dead and B Real went crazy as he realized how Bj always end up getting the upper hand on him. "Put that bitch's clothes back on her. This n*ga some how got my girl and now I'm just finding out she's pregnant. He better pray that don't nothing happens to her. A Hood you and 2 more of y'all keep an eye on this bitch and don't put a mother f*cking hand on her and I mean it."

B Real received a call from Bj bright and early the next morning giving him the instructions on where the meeting place would be and when. B Real was a little uncomfortable about the meeting spot but figured this is the only chance of getting his girl back, so he agreed with it. He just know now that he's going to have to bring his whole team cause there will be a monkey wrench in the game and this time he would be ready.

B Real was on his way to the spot where his guys is holding their hostage when he sees Meaka coming out of the currency exchange on 59yth and Ashland. He pulled on the side of her as she was sticking her key in the driver side door.

"What's up Meaka?" he asks. She turned around and when she saw who it was she dropped her keys on the ground. She bent down to pick them up off the ground, while speaking to him at the same time.

"What's up boo? Why you been ignoring your girl's calls?"

"Shorty, don't play, you know my number is the last number you been trying to call."

"I'm for real boo. I got information that I know you going to love."

"For real, what is it?" he nodded his head signaling for her to come get in the car with him.

She hesitated, but did as she was told, so he wouldn't think she was on some bullshit . As soon as she got in, he pulled off while she gave him the directions to Bj mother's house.

B Real pulled up in front of the house and parked. Meaka sat in the passenger seat nervous as she did not know what was going to happen next. She was expecting him to just make sure it's the house and then take her back to her car and consider the deal finished.

Meaka stared looking around as if she's searching for some thing. "Her car is not out here. She must be at work or something."

"Just get out and go knock on the door. Somebody might be there."

"What am I going to say if someone answer the door?"

"Tell them that you know Bj and that you need to use the phone. It's important. Then call my cell phone and just say a number letting me know how many peoples are in the house."

As Meaka walked up the steps she prayed that no one was there. As she looked around to make sure no one is looking out their windows cause shit might get ugly if someone answers this door.

She knocked on the door, like twice and waited for an answer. No one said anything, so she looked in the direction of B Real and shook her head signaling that there's no answer. He then signaled for her to knock again. She did as she was told but just a little bit harder. This time, as she now figures no one's there.

A minute later, with stilll no answer, she started walking

184

down the stairs. As soon as she reached the bottom stair, the door opens. At the moment, she could have pissed on herself.

"Excuse me , ma'am, you looking for someone?"

She turned around and seem that it was Bj's baby brother who is in 8th grade. "Is Bj here?"

"No, he's not. Who is you?"

"I'm Tameaka. OK, I'll tell him you came by. Is there a number you want to leave for him?"

"Yeah, you have a pen or something to write with?"

"Yeah, give me a second."

"Excuse me, do you mind if I come use your phone. My battery is dead."

""Sure come on in."

Meaka went inside and did as she came to do. She gave him a fake number to leave for Bj, while she made her phone call. She didn't hear anyone else in the house, so she told B Real "one" and then hung up the phone.

She made small talk with his little brother asking him why he's not in school and what's his name. She started heading for the door as she told him, "Well make sure you tell your brother Meaka was looking for him."

"Is it Meaka or Tameaka?"

She paused for a minute as she realized she done f*cked up. "It's Tameaka. I'm just used to people calling me 'Meaka'".

She reached for the door knob and for some reason it was twisting in her hand. She figures it was Bj's other, but when the door came open it was B Real. Her eyes damn near popped out of their sockets, as he came in with his gun in his hand.

185

Leonard didn't know what to expect as he stood there frozen not able to move.

"Get your ass over there next to that little dum ass f*cker!"

"B Real, please don't do this!"

B Real slapped Meaka across the jaw with the gun knocking her to the floor.

"Bitch who told you to say my name? Now get up and find something to tie his ass up."

Meaka got up and did as she was told. She reached for the phone cord but he stopped her.

"Naw, bitch grab that table cloth and rip it in half."

Meaka did as she was told and she and B Real tied Leonard up to the chair. As soon as they was finished, B Real motioned for Meaka to sit in a chair next to Leonard. He then tied her up. She tried to give him a hard time until he put the gun to the back of her head pulling the hammer back letting her know that he wasn't playing.

A knock from the door caught Meaka's attention. She figured it to be someone in Bj's family. B Real walked to the window and peeked out to make sure it was who he was expecting. Before he had come into the house, he had called 2 of his guys to come help him out.

One guy came in and he told the other one to pull the van around to the back. B Real walked over to the phone, picked it up and started dialing on it. As the phone started ringing, his focus was on a picture that was sitting on the china cabinet of Bj when he was young.

He had on a boy scout uniform. Bj picked up knowing that it

wasn't time for his mother ____ to be back from their trip.

"Why you back so early? Who f*ck is this?"

"You don't know my voice, you just talked to me this morning directing things like you're my boss or something."

"What the f*ck you doing in my mother's house? I swear to God that I'm going to chop you up in so many pieces that they gone find a piece everywhere in all 50 states."

"If I was you I would hold fast on the threats Mr. Boy Scout. You look so innocent in this picture. Ha, ha, ha, ha... Enough of the bullshit homie. I got your little brother Leonard tied up in this chair and thank Meaka for the tip on where your moms stay. She also right here tied up. I can hear you doing a 100 trying to get here so I'm gone make it simple. Be looking for my call on our new meeting place." B Real hung up the phone and headed out the back door with Meaka and Leonard.

When Bj made it to his mother's house, he walked in with his gun out and ready to shoot anyone who wasn't supposed to be there. He sees the 2 chairs sitting in the middle of the dining room, so he checked the rest of the house and came up empty. When he came back down the stairs, he felt something slippery on the bottom of his feet. He grabbed a Kleenex off the table and wiped up the liquid from off the floor. He seen it was blood and hoped it wasn't his lil brother's. He tried calling the phone that he's been getting in contact with B Real on, but it kept going straight to voice mail.

Bj notified his team to meet him at headquarters ASAP. Once everyone was there, the meeting started. "Look fellas, we just encountered a serious situation. I know we suppose to meet with B Real today, but its been a change of plan. This bitch name Meaka done told the n*gga where my mom stay and somehow he got my lil brother. I'm waiting on his call to let me know where our new location going to be. I know he's on some type of rat play, so we have to play smart and be extra careful. I can't let anything happen to my lil brother nor Tonya. If everything go smooth and we get both of them back and secure, we kill everyone in sight. I mean everyone. This is where I want every one to be until we get the call. Make sure everyone have their vests on and their guns locked and loaded cause shits about to get messy. I mean real messy!"

Bj and his crew sat in the Mason Hall waiting on the call from B Real. Six hours done passed and still no call. Scrap and Pooka went to pick up the food from Harold's chicken, since it was right down the street. Bj ordered 200 pieces of chicken for everyone to snack on while they waited.

"Aye, Bj, I just saw J Hood come out the back with 3 people with pillow cases over their heads. I'm following them now up 69th street going towards Racine. What you want us to do?"

"Keep following them and let me know where they stop at. Me and the team is on our way in that direction. Don't do nothing. Just keep an eye on them," was Bj's order.

"OK, make sure you bring us some more steel."

"I already got it."

Scrap followed them all the way to Parkway Housing Complex. When they made it to the back of the complex, there were 10 Ford Taurus parked back there waiting for them. Pooka called Bj and let him know their location.

Bj said he should be there in 10 minutes. Pooka interrupted him with the news that all the cars, including the minivan were pulling off, so to stand by cause this not the meeting place.

J Hood and his guys pulled up to a warehouse where 2 guards were posted up by the entrance way. The garage door came up and all the cars and the minivan pulled in. Pooka and Scrap watched from a block away.

"Yo, Bj, we're on 57th and State, but dude ___ pulled into a warehouse garage on 58th and State. It's 2 guards posted at the garage door with A.K.'s . What you want to do?"

"Just stay there. I'm going to get some of the real shit we got from Matt in Indiana. By that time dude bitch ass should be calling me. Ride past the warehouse and see if it's a way we can get in through the back or where we can post our team up at. Aye, let me hit you back. This that n*gga calling me right now."

"What the f*cks up?"

"Whoa, this ain't the way you talk to someone who have something valuable of yours."

"See that's where you got things f*cked up cause we're even and I'm tired of waiting so I hope yo ready to swap within the next eight hours cause if you're not, then we both can add 2 more to our belts."

"Well, you can add 3 to your with that skank bitch."

"You got a lot of balls to be just saying f*ck your blood brother. I don't think your mother would like to hear how her baby boy ended up in the dirt."

"Let us deal with that, but how would your mother feel when she find out that her only son was killed but the only thing they found was his head cause that's exactly what's going to happen when I catch you." Click. Bj hung up the phone in B Real's face.

He then called team Red Rum and told them where to meet at and that the light done turned green.

"Hello, yeah. OK I'll see you when I get there. Make sure that n*gga, he seems like he got a trick up his sleeve, but my sleeves are much longer this time!:

B Real called Bj back and told him "3 hours, 58th and State, I'll be waiting," and hung up the phone.

Bj and team RedRum posted up in the back of the building, while others sat in their cars scattered out. Pooka and Scrap waited for B Real to arrive so that the 2 people that were sitting in the alley 2 blocks down can come ram the garbage truck through the front garage door.

B Real pulled up in a black on black late model Hummer. Ten minutes later Scrap and 3 other guys accompanied Bj inside the building, while Pooka waited outside with 3 guys guarding Monica until they're called to bring her in.

Once inside, the 2 guards, with the AK 47's ushered Bj and his crew to the fifth floor where the transaction is to be made. The guard that was in the front opened the door to his right and stood to the side, so they could enter.

"Y'all better turn on some lights first before we enter." As soon as Bj had said that each of his men upped their weapons ready to attack.

"There's another door we have to go through about 10 steps ahead."

"Well, I think you need to be walking ahead first to open the

190

door cause this is the farthest we're going until we can see."

The guard went ahead and opened the door to a big room that looks like it could be a parking garage.

Once they made it to the door Scrap looked to his left then his right and saw B Real and about 10 of his guys standing off to the side.

"Come on in fellas. What y'all going to stay at the door all day?" was B Real's greeting.

As Bj and his guys walked in they noticed that there were 5 doors in view and instantly anticipated that other men were behind them doors.

B Real looked at his watch and said, "I see you're one minute early. The earlier, the better."

Scrap and J Hood had a stare off, as if eyes could kill.

"So where's my package at?"

"It's close by. What about mine?"

B Real snapped his fingers signaling for his guys to go get Tonya and Meaka. As they brought Tonya through the door she was giving up a fight trying to get loose. Her hands were tied behind her back with what looked like a sock in her mouth. Meaka was not giving up a fight, as if she knew she was going to make it free.

"That's not the whole package. As you can see, you could of killed that grimey ass bitch Meaka, but where's my lil brother at?"

"He's close by as well, but I need to get my package first."

"That wasn't the plan."

"We never did say what the plan was. I just told you where

191

to meet at and what time."

"Look here homie, you better watch the way you speak the words out your mouth before it get ugly in here."

"This not your place to be throwing threats my dude. You're on my turf."

"I wouldn't care who turf we're on, but you're not going to talk to me any type of way. I'm a boss, not a soldier."

"Right now, I'm the boss in this camp and we gone do it my way or get bloody."

Bj's guys upped their weapons as well as B Real's guys, but more guys started coming out of the other doors, just as Bj had figured.

"I see you had your back up plan ready, huh? But I already expected that."

"So what's it going to be? You gone call for my package or what?"

"Like I told you, either you gone show me my lil brother or my mother will be legally rich off his and my insurance. You make the choice."

Bj and B Real had a stare off while both teams waited for the word from their boss to light up the room like the 4th of July. B Real broke the silence first as he antipcate seeing if MOinca is really pregnant.

"Go get that lil bastard before my patience runs out."

One of his guys did as he was told in 0.2 seconds but he went in a different door than they went in the first time.

"Now, I think you need to get on your phone, walky talky or what ever you're using to make your demands and get me my package."

As soon as Leonard came through the door, Bj got on his phone and told Pooka to bring her up to the 5th floor.

Down stairs as soon as Pooka got off the phone, he chirped team RedRum and let them know that the 5th floor was the spot and to wait for the command.

Pooka and 3 more guys pulled up to the garage and waited for the guard to get the OK to let them in. Once inside they got out with Monica, tied her hands behind her back and mouth stuffed also and followed the guards up to the 5th floor.

Pooka and Monica came through the door first and instantly B Real could tell she was pregnant. Then following them were the 3 guys who was with them.

"Bring her to the front, so we can handle our shit and get the f*ck up out of here" Bj said. "Now, send me my people and you can get your baby mama."

"First let Janet go and then I'll give you these 2?"

"Who the hell is Janet? Her name is Monica."

"Where the hell you get Monica from? Bay tell this n*gga your name."

"Trust me, blood I know her name in fact, I know everything about her. How about you?"

"That's my girl. Of course I know her, but her damn name ain't Monica."

"Whatever homie, Give me my people and you and your girl can live a life happily ever after or we can just get it crackin in here and may the best man live."

B Real signaled for his men to free Tonya but Bj stopped

him. "Naw, bro. Let me get my lil brother first. I don't know why you even still got her anyway. She's just a jump off. Don't get me wrong, though, the p*ssy is fire, but not fire enough for me to put my life on the line coming up in here."

Tonya looked at him crazy cause she couldn't tell whether he was for real or shooting a bluff.

Outside Tater Bean listened on his cell phone as the conversation went on inside the warehouse. Pooka had called his phone before he went in, so that team RedRum could hear the word to come in and assist them.

The garbage truck started heading towards the warehouse, as they realized that they needed to be getting close as time starts winding down. Mystery sat in the passenger side of the garbage truck as Coco drove. Once in front of the warehouse, she came up with a plan to get inside without making any noise outside. "Stop the truck and follow me. First take off everything but your panties and bra."

Both girls got nearly naked and exited the truck heading in the direction of the guards swishing their hips as if they were on the runway for Tyra's Next Top Model. As soon as they were in breathing range, their expertise kicked in. Coco took her man with no problem, while Mystery wrestled with her guard. Somehow he knocked Mystery down and the AK 47 was pointed at her head telling her not to move until Coco gave him a light chop to the neck, knocking him out cold.

"Thanks, I owe you one." Mystery said.

Coco said in her Belizian accent, "That's what friends fa."

The rest of team RedRum pulled up hopping out of their

cars. "Y'all boys too late. Me and my gal could be dead by now."

"Girl come on, let's get upstairs before it's too late."

"Meka tell the boys the truth."

"Just come on."

B Real signaled for Leonard to be untied but not released until his Janet was untied. "I think you need to be untying my girl as well."

"What? You think you running things here?"

Pooka started untieing Monica and letting her walk over to B Real as Leonard came over to the side where Bj was. Once that transaction was done the rest of Bj's team RedRum and the 2 girls came through the door with their guns drawn, as Scrap, Pooka and the rest of the guys upped their weapons, as well as B Real's team.

Both sides stood there with their guns out anxious to start blazing. "So I can see now that the deal is done, y'all ready to get it popping up in here?"

"Oh, the deal ain't completely done. I gave you 2. Now let me get my girl."

"I thought you didn't want her."

"I was expecting to get me another shot of that good stuff."

"Well do that on your own time. Right now you're on my time and time is ticking."

"Well, I am a man of my word. Let that bitch go Hood."

Hood kissed her on the neck and shoved her over into Bj's arms.

Some more of B Real's guys came out of the doors on the

195

side pointing their weapons. Bj seen that his team was outnumbered but stilll felt the need to get things poppin.

By this time, Leonard was escorted down the stairs by Mystery and Coco, while Tonya retrieved 2 pistols from the guys.

"Now, since we're here, we can either get to the real point at hand, or we can kill each other right here in this warehouse."

"Tell your guys to put their weapons down and we can go off to one of my rooms and talk like real men."

"Naw, bro, we gone put them down, when your team put theirs down." B Real signaled his men, then Bj did the same.

"So, where is this room at that you want to do the man to man at?"

"Over here, you first."

"What's with all this you first shit like you're on something slick?"

"What you're scared or something?"

"Never scared, just safe."

"Well, you can only bring 2 of your flunkies and he rest can stay in here." Bj signaled for Tonya and Scrap to join him.

"Oh, I see she was more than what you showed for her."

"What you expected me to front my hand? You know I'm smarter that that."

"Now, I know."

B Real, J Hood and one of his top soliders was on one side of the table, while Bj, Scrap and Tonya stood on the other side.

"Soo B Real, first let me ask you why did we have to go thought all this blood shed just to have this meeting? We could

196

have been making more money than we are now."

"I'm stilll making money and it ain't gone stop."

"What good is it if you can't enjoy it?"

"Is you making a threat?"

"Naw, that goes for both of us. It's just that we both lost a lot of soldiers all because of what? This meeting we're having now, that I've been trying to have?"

"See you and your brother took our blocks and we wasn't going to just sit around and let y'all enjoy it. So that's where the war kicked in at."

"First, I didn't take or help take anything. That first run in we had at the club, it was trying to return them back, but you was really feeling yourself and wanted to be disrespectful."

"Hey, what you expect? You was in my house trying to make demands."

"I sent a message to met with you before the club, but never got an answer so when I found out that you was at the club, I came to meet with you."

"Enough of all the explaining. You here, now Talk."

"OK your man's Tear Drop is gone and my brother is gone, so that leaves us in charge. I know you selling crack and weed and I'm selling dope crack and weed. I'm willing to call a peace treaty and give you half of your land back, but you can't sell no more weed and I'm gone stop my men from selling crack that way you control the city on crack."

"That sounds good, but I'm gone need all my blocks back. Come on now. You got to meet me half way."

"I don't think that's going to work cause you're going to

197

stilll be too close to me."

"That shouldn't matter cause we're calling a peace treaty."

"So what happens if he peace treaty gets broken?"

"Let's see…if the treaty gets broken then the person who broke it have to…shit, that's a hard question there. I didn't even think about that one."

"I say who ever breaks the treaty, then the opponent gets the pleasure of taking his life right in front of his boss and to top it off it's a $10,000 fine. So what you say?"

"I kind of like that deal, but let's make it worth our pockets and make it $50,000."

"You talking big money and that's what I like. It's a deal!"

B Real reached out to shake Bj's hand and Bj just looked at him with a smirk on his face, as he said, "It's a peace treaty, but don't get it twisted. We're not friends." Then he turned around to leave out the door. But not without forgetting to let B Real know one more thing, "by the way them 2 guards you had at the door downstairs, they're dead. But it happened before our peace treaty.

B Real just stood there with a mug on his face as Bj just let him know that he got the last lick.

Bj walked over to where the rest of his guys were and they then followed him out towards the door. Just as he was about to walk through the door, Meaka called out to him, "Bj, please take me with you, please. I'm sorry for all I have done. Don't leave me here. He's going to kill me. Please take me with you. Please!"

Bj turned around in her direction and had a look on his face as if he was contemplating on taking her with him until B Real signaled for J Hood to take her out of her misery and without questioning he put his gun to her temple and blew all her brain fragments right on the floor then looked over at Bj, as if he couldn't wait to do him the same way. Bj smirked at their stupidity, then proceeded out the door.

As soon as Bj stepped a foot out the warehouse, Mystery and Coco was parked right at the entrance with Leonard in the backseat. He hopped in the back seat while everyone else returned towards their cars to drop him off at his car so he and his lil brother can ride alone and have a long talk as he takes him back home. Well, to his grandmother's house.

"How you feeling, lil bro."

"I'm cool, but what's going on with them guys and why did they try to kidnap me?"

"You see you won't understand."

"Yes, I will, just tell me."

"OK, we have a war goin on out here and as you can see that guy B Real is the one who I'm at war with, but as of right now, there's a peace treaty. There's no telling how long that's going to last."

"Who was them girls with no clothes on that I was in the car with?"

"Them some trusted friends of mine, but what I want to say to you is you got to make sure don't nobody find out about this lil incident. I mean no one, not even Ben."

"Can I have a gun, so that if they try to take me again I can protect myself?"

"NO! You can not and I want you to forget about everything that happened cause it will never happen again. So focus on your school work and I'm going to make sure you don't want for nothing in life."

"OK, Bj, you got my word on that!"

"Is you hungry?"

"Yeah, I'm starving!"

"What you want to eat?"

"Uh, uh, some McDonald's, yeah that's what I want."

Bj chirped White Boy and told him that he was stopping at Mickey D's and then he's going to drop his lil brother off at his grandmother's house and for him to lead everybody to the Mason Hall and wait for him to get there.

Bj and Leonard sat in the restaurant eating and talking about the good and bad of life and also Leonard's small and long term goals. Once they was finished eating, he dropped him off and promised him that he would take him to the mall tomorrow.

When Bj arrived at the Mason Hall he was happy to see all the cars that was parked out there. Even Mystery and Coco's car was parked out there, so tonight would be a good night.

As he was walking up the stairs, he could hear everyone making small talk with each other until he entered the room. That's when the applause came form all his soldiers. Even some were whistling as if victory has been set.

Bj made his way through the crowd and up to his podium. He raised his hand to quiet the noise down, so he can take the floor. Everyone followed suit and listened on as if Jessie Jackson was speaking himself.

200

"First, I'd like to thank you all for sticking by each other's side so that this task that we had tonight came out our way and safely at that. Yeah things could have went sour, but because we are thinkers and not rascals, we were able to come out on top and also come to a conclusion where the blood flow can come to a halt. And also more money can be made. Now look, while we were in the room and you all were out in the warehouse, ready for war, we came to a one wasy conclusion and that is that we're at a peace treaty right now and I want you all to know that I love each and everyone as if you are my own flesh and blood and you all showed me the same love, but we have to and mean every word I'm about to say, we have to be on the same page at all times cause there is a consequence to anyone. I mean anyone who breaks the treaty. What we came up with is that whatever side breaks the treaty, then that person will be executed by the other side how ever they want to and the boss have to be there to watch it. plus there's a $50,000 fine also. SO I ask that you all don't put me and yourself in that position and I trust that you won't because we are thinkers and know what..." he pointed to the crowd and they responded by saying "Rascals". He requested it 3 more time to make sure everyone understood, then he took the floor again.

"Also I'm giving him half of the land we took from him back.

Some of the people in the crowd looked back and forth at each other, as if they couldn't understand what was going on, until he continued talking. "I know y'all thinking like what the f*ck but everything is done for a reason. By me having the dope and the weed on lock, so he's not to sell any dope, weed or x pills and we're not to sell any crack in his land or also our land. Trust me when I tell you that our money count is about to shoot sky high. I got this new connect on the pills for dirt cheap. Now everyone who was selling crack can either take the weed or the pills as a substitute. Now the land that I'm giving him back is already upon that , so we don't need that and I'm giving him Mike-Mike's spot on Carpenter. But everything else we keeping. Everyone has up to next Friday to get rid of their work and then, that's it. If anyone has a problem with everything that's going into effect right now, then speak now cause once we leave this hall, then I'm taking it as everyone is on the same page.

He took a few minutes for everyone to make up their mind then he spoke again. "OK, now that's what I want to see. everyone's on the same page. Before we leave tonight, I know everyone who don't know been wanting to know who is these 2 females. Well, her name is Mystery and her actions is everything that her name says and this is Coco and just put it like this, They're our secret weapons and its more of them. Now I reserved all the VIP sections at the River Center for us tonight. So let's go celebrate tonight to a new beginning and a never ending movement."

The cheers started up again, but this time you could feel the love from it.

Bj Pulled up in his brother's silver Porsche and all eyes were on him. He jumped out wearing a white Coogi fitted ha with an all white Coogi jogging suit and some crispy all while low tops Air Force Ones He walked up to the bouncer at the door, shook his hand and walked straight in.

As soon as he made it through the door, the DJ announced that he was in the building and the crowd went wild. As he walked through the crowd towards the VIP section everyone made a clear path so it wouldn't be any mistake. The closer he got the more visual his crew became. He saw his boy, White Boy, posted front and center, but to his right, he couldn't help seeing Tonya dressed in a one piece body suit that made every curve she had stick out like a sore thumb and instantly his piece got hard a hell that he had to put his hand in front of him to hide the bulge in his pants.

He greeted White Boy and then walked over to Tonya to acknowledge her beauty. "You looking real gorgeous tonight!"

"So are you in your all white."

"To me that's a sign to let people know that you don't want to be touched."

"Now you know a man like me always wants to be touched."

"Yeah I know, but I'm stilll mad at you."

"What did I do?"

"I wonder if that was Sheena that they had instead of me, would you have played your cards like that?"

"That wasn't nothing for you to get mad about. See if I would have showed any weakness then we probably wouldn't be having this discussion and you know that."

"I'm just making sure that we are still on the same page."

"You got me thinking about changing my plans for tonight."

"Don't lie like that. A woman in my shoes couldn't sleep without saying some thing."

"That's why I like you girl."

"I can't wait till you start loving me."

Before Bj could even respond to her last statement, the crowd was in an up roar and when he turned around to see what was going on the crowd had parted a line heading right in his direction. He couldn't believe his eyes as 2 females took the whole club's attention as they entered.

Once they reached the VIP section, Tonya couldn't help but like what she saw also. She always dreamed about her being in a hot and sweaty escapade with the women before her eyes, but never took the time to shoot her shot because of her cockiness, but tonight she's going to try her luck on a threesome.

"I see someone trying to take my shine," Bj said as he sized Mystery and Coco up. Both ladies were dressed in some tight fitting spandex that had their p*ssy print, showing, as if they got camel in their blood, with some shirts that came just below their breast where you can see the bottom of their titties.

"Now, boo why would I do that? I'm trying to share the spot light with you , not take it."

"Then if that's so the, what's mine is yours." Tonya gave Mystery a big hug but you could sense a little jealousy, but only Bj knew. She then gave Coco a hug then they took their seats to enjoy the rest of the night.

White Boy walked over to Coco and asked her to dance, but she shot him down. She told him that he could keep her company for night and maybe all morning, He jumped on that ASAP as he flopped down next to her and threw his arms around her shoulder and said, "Shit, I'll take that over a dance anytime."

204

"I bet you would," Bj added.

The crew sat in the VIP section drinking Rose Moet for the rest of the night. Tonya was sitting on the right side of Bj while Mystery sat on the left. Both ladies had been playing footsy and rubbing on his legs and penis under the table all night and even touched each other's hands while trying to rub his penis at the same time.

Mystery spoke up, "Can y'all excuse me for a second? This champagne is trying to run out of me."

"Yeah, me too," Tonya said. This was her opportunity to come at Mystery.

Both ladies got up and walked to the ladies room. Bj watched as both women switched it up as if they're walking the runway. He fantasized for a quick second on what it would be like to have both of them in bed at the same time, but the quicker the thought came, it disappeared because the type of women both of them are, and their occupation.

Tonya walked in first and Mystery couldn't help but to like the way Tonya's ass was jiggling with every step. Tonya assumed that Mystery would look, so she made sure that if so it would be a sight to see. Tonya knocked on one of the stalls and didn't get an answer, so she went in to take care of her business. Mystery knocked on the next stall door but there was a female sitting on the toilet in a nod from hell like she just snorted some dope fresh off the plate. Mystery banged on the door to snap the girl out of her nod and the girl jumped up as if her life was in danger. Shit it caught Mystery off guard also, but her instinct kicked in so fast as 3 razors popped out her mouth and rested on her tongue as if they were waiting on a command to strike.

The lady spoke up as she flushed the toilet and proceeded to walk out the stall, "I'm sorry ma'am. I musta fell the sleep in here."

Mystery looked at her like she was crazy as she tried to act like Mystery was new to the world not know why the lady was sleep on the toilet.

Mystery was bout to use the toilet but the smell that the lady left behind was not sitting right with her stomach and hen Mystery heard the toilet flushing in the stall where Tonya was. She decided to use that stall instead.

"Girl, I'm glad you came out cause I was going to either piss on myself or bust in your stall and tell you to scoot over cause home girl, who just came out of this stall smell like something died in her or something and I was not bout to sit in there."

"I don't blame you. Hoes in here trying to impress these n*ggas and forget about their ladyness"

"I feel you girl," Mystery said from the stall.

Tonya stood in the mirror acting as if she was fixing her appearance but was really waiting on Mystery to come out so she can shoot her shot from what Mystery said about sharing the toilet gave Tonya a lil hope that she can pull it off. Tonya heard the toilet flush and knew that her task was here.

"Ooh shit, that felt so good, " Mystery said as she headed over to the sink next to Tonya to wash her hands and fix her clothes.

"I bet it did girl. That bubble have a bitch pissing like Lake

206

Michigan."

"Who you telling?"

"Girl, you looking real hot in that outfit tonight!"

"I must say the same about your appearance."

"Naw, girl, you really killing shit tonight. You had all the men's attention and even a lot of bitches too screaming rape with their eyes."

"I know girl, did you see them? It is a lot of fine brothers in this bitch tonight and a couple of females as well but in order for a bitch to get a taste of this she better be bad as hell and got a n*gga with her that's gone kill this shit." she said as she patter her mound or should I say her camel toe.

Tonya looked down at her p*ssy with lust in her eyes and Mystery didn't miss the look that Tonya had on her face as well. "Girl, you think we can gang rape Bj tonight?"

"Yeah, I think we can pull it off. My place or yours?"

"I got a room at the Drake hotel for tonight cause I was planning on getting my back knocked out but now it's goin go to be more exciting with a third party, Mystery said as she got closer up on Tonya and tongued her like it was no tomorrow while stilll holding the razors in her mouth. Tonya couldn't help herself so she stuck her hands down the front of Mystery's pants and flicked at her clit, then stuck her finger in to see how wet it gets. Mystery let out a light moan as she tried to move her body as if she was riding a dick.

Tonya pulled her finger out and stuck it in her mouth to taste the flavor. "Mmm, vanilla, splash is my favorite,"

Two females walked in and saw how close Tonya and

Mystery was and knew that something kinky was going on. Mystery looked at the females and said in a seductive way, "You want to taste this too?" Both females turned around and ran back out of the washroom. "Girl, lets get out of here and go get our man for tonight and blow this hot dog stand."

When Tonya and Mystery made it back to the VIP section, Bj said, "Is y'all alright? I thought I had to come in there and save y'all cause of how long y'all was in there."

"We cool, in fact, we ready to leave in a few minutes," Mystery said as she nodded at Tonya to let her inform Bj of tonight's affairs.

Tonya leaned over and whispered in Bj's ear and he looked over at Mystery, as if he couldn't believe that was just said to him. Mystery shook her head up and down to confirm so.

White Boy sensed what was going on and asked Coco was she bouncing with him for the night. She looked over at Mystery and Mystery gave her the OK that she is cool with them separating for the night.

White Boy stood up and embraced Bj and said, "Alright, big bro. I'm gone catch you tomorrow or maybe the next day after that cause I see you got both of your hands full."

"Alright, lil bro cause Coco look like she bout her thang as well."

Both men went around hollering a the rest of the crew before they left.

Bj, Tonya and Mystery rode to the hotel in his brother's Porsche. He started to let one of the ladies drive, but thought about as if it was his car he wouldn't want his brother letting a female drive his shit and plus he didn't want to get anything in motion in the car cause he's going to need all the energy he got for these 2 freaks.

Tonya and Mystery rode in the back seat and decided to start early while Bj drove. He almost had 3 different accidents cause he was trying to drive and watch the show that was going on in he back seat. His phone started ringing and as he look at the caller ID, noticed it was wifey. He decided to tell them to hold fast with all the moaning but decided to turn the radio up to drown out the noise.

"Hello my beauty queen. What is you doing up so late?"

"You know I haven't' heard from you all day. How can I go to sleep without hearing your voice and also making sure you all right."

"You know daddy alright girl."

"Why you got the radio up so loud?"

"Cause I just left the club and Scrap and White Boy had a little too much to drink, so I refuse to let them drive home so I'm dropping them off at a room then I'm heading home."

"I miss you bay and I'm ready to come home. My kitty is purring for you."

"I miss you even more and I can't wait for you to get here in 2 more days. Shit I was thinking about sending for you early."

"What's that noise I just heard in the background bay?"

"That's Scrap imitating some hing a stripper did to White Boy."

"I wonder what they did and know what, I'm going to talk to you in the morning. You trying to blow my high."

209

"I'm sorry bay, I was just joking."

"No, you weren't."

"Yes, I was"

"Good night Sheena. I'll talk to you in the morning."

"You better not hang this phone up…"

"Good night Sheena."

"Bryant, you better not…"

and the phone went dead in her ear. Bj turned it off completely cause he knew she was going to call back.

Bj pulled up to the front of the hotel and the valet was right there to get his keys. The valet just stood there cause of the episode that was taking place in the back seat. He coughed twice to break the ladies out of their trance but the show kept on going. Bj stood behind the guy laughing but not loud enough for the guy to hear him cause of the expression on his face as Tonya's moans got louder and louder.

Bj spoke up, "Ladies, let's make our way to the room. I want some as well. Mystery and Tonya took a few seconds to cool off so they can head into the hotel and not look like some hoes or sluts. Mystery got out the car first followed by Tonya. As she stopped to fix her clothes, she looked down and saw that the guy's penis was bout to bust out of his pants if he saw a minute more of the episode. Tonya being crazy as she is had the balls to thump the tip of his penis with force as she told him, "too bad he's at attention for nothing, unless you going to use your hand," and kept walking to catch up with Mystery and Bj.

While in the elevator, Bj stuck his hand in Mystery's pants and was playing with her p*ssy, while Tonya pulled Mystery's

left tit out and started sucking on her nipple with full force. Instantly Mystery came hard in her pants that now showed a wet spot as if she pissed on herself.

Bj then switched to Tonya to see if he can make the same thing happen to her before the elevator makes it to they stop which is only 3 more floors up. As they were reaching the last floor, Tonya was moaning and saying that she was cumming and as soon as the elevator came to a stop and the door came open, Bj looked down at Tonya's p*ssy area and watched as the wetness appeared the same as Mystery's.

"Let's go ladies cause I'm bout to get the bed wetter than that spot that's in y'all pants."

As soon as the room was open, clothes were flying everywhere. Tonya pushed Bj on the bed and started longing him to death while Mystery went straight for his dick and swallowed it whole. Mystery was moving his dick in and out of her mouth as if she was born without tonsils. Tonya felt the way Bj was moving as if he was enjoying himself and had to look down and see what performance Mystery was doing and it shocked her eyes the way Mystery was sucking on his dick with professional rhythm, so she slid down and joined Mystery by inserting his balls in her mouth and Bj went crazy and exploded like a volcano on Mystery and Tonya's faces.

Tonya and Mystery started kissing and fondling with each other's breasts and then Tonya pushed her down on the bed and spread her legs. As she took a dive head first into Mystery's neat shaved p*ssy, she had to use both of her hands to keep her p*ssy lips spread so she can have a clear way to her pearl tongue cause

211

of how fat Mystery's p*ssy was.

Bj get up and positioned himself behind Tonya, as she had her ass tilted up ready for him to enter her from behind. He plunged in her with so much force that she put extra pressure on to Mystery's pearl tongue, which Mystery moan so loud as if she had the dick in her. "Oooohh, shit, yeah!" The more Bj pounded away, the more Tonya sucked her clit and the louder Mystery's moaning and screaming became. ""I'm coming hard, like a mother f*cker!" Mystery said, as she dragged each word. Tonya tried to keep sucking on Mystery, but couldn't cause she was also coming hard herself, as Bj dicked her down with all 9 ½ inches nonstop. Mystery crawled from under Tonya and moved Tonya out of the way so she can get the feel of the dick also and lay her tongue game down on Tonya, as if she is competing to be in a porn movie. Instead of Bj going right in Mystery, he walked over and put his dick into Tonya's mouth, so that she can get a taste of her own juices and also clean his dick on the sneak tip. Once has was rock hard and satisfied with her job he got behind Mystery and started licking her p*ssy while she licked on Tonya. Mystery moved her ass around in the same motion as he was licking her so that she can get the full pleasure whil stilll holding onto Tonya as she tried to run from the Tonya lashing that Mystery had. She always knew that her tongue was a gift to her.

Mystery and Tonya both started shaking as they reached their orgasms at the same time. Well pleased with his work, Bj rearranged the scenery by laying on his back and having Tonya to sit on his face, as Mystery hops on him and rides his life away. Instead of Mystery just handling her business on the dick she decided to lean forward and lick Tonya's ass and ride the dick at the same time and 10 seconds into it Tonya came like Niagara Falls all over Bj's face. SO much that she almost drowned him. Mystery was doing her thing as she was moaning and groaning and holding on tight to Tonya's ass cheeks as she was coming so hard. She felt Bj's dick head swell up inside her and knew he was bout to explode in her, so she raised up off him and tried to suck the well dry as she swallowed every drop of nut out of him.

Bj was drained, but that didn't stop Tonya and Mystery as they collided into each other's body, as if they were in love. Bj rolled up a blunt and sat there smoking as he watched the girls in a sixty-nine position for what seemed like forever. He wanted to join them again for one more round, but his dick was hurting cause of the quadruple nuts he has busted. So he would have to wait until tomorrow to thrash both of them again.

The next morning before the birds can even start chirping, the three were at it again and even ended up in the shower before Bj left to handle his early morning affairs. He is supposed to meet his brother's broyer then take his lil brother shopping like he promised.

Bj bought his lil brother 3 pairs of shoes and 2 outfits to go with each. He wanted to spend more time with him but had some important business to take care of today. So he dropped him back off right in front of his grandmother's house. As Leonard got out and was bout to go through the gate, Bj called him back to the car and gave him $200 in twentys. He told him to give half of that to his cousin Ben and he would see him later. He waited until Leonard was completely in the house before he pulled off.

213

Bj made all his rounds through the land. He had Scrap following him, as he stopped at all his spots and had Scrap collect the cocaine and money. They replaced it with ten bundles of dope. Once he made all his stops, he had collected over a key and a half of cocaine back from his crew and going to send it to his shorty in Minnesota to get off and also make a huge profit off it cause the prices is double out of town. After everything was done, they shot out west to McArthur's for some soul food and also meet with his new connect to discuss some prices on the x pills.

Bj had a large order of beef short ribs with a side order of macaroni, greens and sweet potatoes, while Scrap ordered the meat loaf with gravy and smothered potatoes and sweet peas on the side. Both of them smashed their food like they hadn't eaten in years. Once they was finished, they sat in the car smoking on a blunt waiting for Kato to show up.

Bj met Kato through his brother since he's been in jail. Kato is a Latin King from Humbolt Park who is the son of one of the most known kings throughout the United States.

Kato pulled up in a F 150 sitting on what looks like some 30 inch chrome five point star rims. He was listening to Pitbull. He hopped out of the truck but left it running cause he had a bad ass Puerto Rican in the truck with him, who will give Jennifer Lopez a run for her money.

"What's up Carona? How's the world treating you, bro?"

"I can't call it moe man just trying to make it day by day."

"I feel you, get on in. Let me rap to you for a minute."

"What's that y'all smoking, bro? Some backyard boogie?"

"Yeah, it's some regular."

"You want to hit that shit?"

"Naw, I don't smoke that type of weed, but hold on for a second. I just got some new shit in we call Purple Haze."

"That's that shit that dude Camron be smoking."

"Yeah, bro that shit is fine bro."

"Aye, Maria, bring me that bag of purp out the stash."

Maria got the weed and came up to the car and passed it to Kato with a book of rolling papers too.

"I got an extra blunt right here Kato."

"Naw, bro, you got to smoke this in papers bro."

"Is that it papi?"

'Naw, turn around boo."

Maria turned around and you would have thought she had some black in her the way her ass cheeks was hanging out of them booty shorts she had on. Kato smacked her on her ass and it shook like she had Jello in her family. "Now go get back in the truck Mami."

And without hesitation, she was off and running.

"That's your girl, Kato?"

"Naw, she's just a jump off. Why you want that?"

Bj didn't want to feel thirsty, so he said, "Naw, I want to let me man hit that". But he really wanted to tear her a new booty hole.

"We having a get together Saturday. Why don't you and your guys slide through. We first cousins. You're always welcome bro."

"I'll be there. Count me in."

Kato lit the joint up, hit it twice and then passed it to Bj. He took one pull off it like he was smoking on a blunt and damn near coughed his lungs up and when Scrap took a puff off it, he did the same thing.

"Y'all better stop smoking that bullshit bro and get used to this real shit bro. Me got a lot of his shit bro."

Bj was trying to say some thing, but he couldn't stop coughing long enough for the words to come out.

Kato got out and grabbed 2 bottles of water and gave one to Bj and one to Scrap to clear their throats from burning. When he got back in, he tossed a bottle of pills that was all different colors on Bj's lap.

"This how they come Kato?"

"Yeah, bro, plus I can put any symbol on them that you want."

"Yeah, bro, so this what them n*ggas and hoes be going crazy for, huh?"

"Yeah this what keep them rollin. You heard what Gucci be saying."

"What's the ticket on these?"

"They cost 20 per pill on the block but I get them for $2 a pill and 100 come in the jar. So I'm going to charge you $5 a pill, so we can make money and if you spending over ten stacks, then I'm going to have your logs put on there for a dollar a bottle and check this out, I'm gone front you what ever you buy bro, for half price. You can't beat that."

"No disrespect Kato, but I don't do the credit. My money

phat right now."

"Well, you better get you an accountant cause your money bout to be doing somersaults cause you're the only one I'm selling to in Chicago. So stay loyal and you won't want for anything bro. That's my word, bro."

"Well, let me get on the road with this, so I can get this shit poppin. What you want for this bottle here?"

"That's your sample bro. From your brother Nuke and my brother."

"Just get at me and stay at me."

"I got you Kato and one more thing, what's up with that Purple Haze?"

"You can keep this ounce as well, but take it easy before you die on me."

"I got you Kato. I'll give you a call tomorrow evening and I'm going to see my brother in a couple of days. You want to meet me down there?"

"Just call my phone, bro. We can do that."

"Alright cuzo, Amor."

"Amor, Kato."

Bj and Scrap was riding through the hood when they saw Coodinc, Jessica, and Doctoria coming out the liquor store on Ashland. He pulled over to make small talk with them and then gave them all a pill a piece and told them they had to pop it right there and to call him in an hour to let him know what's to them. Them being some pill popping animals, they didn't hesitate to pop them and they was free at that. Doctoria had a quarter juice in her hand that she had just opened and the 3 of them used that same juice to pop their pill. Not one thing about the 3 was that they didn't care about showing that they was some hood hoes.

Bj received a call from Doctoria and the other girls 10 minutes later asking when and where was he going to open up at cause his shit is poppin. He told them that Saturday he goin to have a pass out from 10:00 am to 12:00 noon and then he would be selling them for $10 a pill. 24 hours and if they don't have a squirrel on them, then they're not his and to let him know.

The next 3 days was good to him. He didn't think that the pills was going to bring so much traffic like its doing so he took the weed and dope off his main block and only selling pills on that block. He put the dope on the next block cause it was time to move it around. Plus on the second day of opening, his dope line was booming. He had to put the dope line on one side of the block and the pills on the other side. That day he made $40,000 off his dope and $5,000 off the pills. The neighbors was tripping cause of the traffic in front of their houses. SO he went by each house and gave the owner $100 and told them that as long as they bare with him and ride with him, he will pay half of wha their rent every month and everyone agreed.

Bj walked into the court room Tuesday morning feeling good for some reason. He sat in the second row waiting for his brother's broyer to come in so he can get a chance to talk to him before court starts.

Ten minutes later, Nuke's broyer comes in from out the back instead of the front. This means that he's been here already and was in the back talking to Nuke. He looked in Bj's direction with

218

a smile on his face then winked his left eye, which means that something good is about to happen today.

The bailiff stepped up and said, "All rise in this court room for the Honorable Judge Harpotime."

The judge came in and took a seat behind his desk and spoke, "Good morning to everyone," which let all know he was in a good mood.

He then went to calling names as if he has something to do today and will not be in the court room all day.

After 2 misdemeanor cases, he looked over to the bench where all the public defenders were sitting and told them that if their clients here for a misdemeanor that he's giving them time consider served so they don't have to come out here. All the public defenders started shifting through their folders then were heading to the back bull pens to give their clients the news. The states attorney looked as if they had an attitude but, hey, what can they do?

The next person came up was facing an arm violence and was trying to get his bond from $5,000 to walk to at last $20,000 but the judge only dropped it to $30,000. Then a few more peoples was called who had simple possession of controlled substances. Two of them copped out for 2 years' probation and the other one said he was going to trial.

Next up was Nuke, He came out with a baby fro as if he was growing his hair back. His broyer stepped up on the side of him as the judge asked what's going on today.

"Well your Honor, we here today for a bond hold to be lifted off my client."

219

"Oh, I remember this case. Aint' the state supposed to have some paper work stating that this man shouldn't get a bond?"

"Your Honor, I know I was supposed to have the paper work today, but the chief of the gang intelligence won't be back till next week, so I'm asking you for one more week continuance."

"Objection, your Honor. My client's wife is due any day now and the state has had 2 weeks to prove their statement but they can't."

"Excuse me for one minute here, " the judge cut in. "I'm not bout to go through this again this week. I'm going to lift your bond, but I'm putting you on home monitoring and if you have a job like you say, then when you present the paperwork from your boss, signed and notarized then you would have movement to work. But until then you would have to abide by the rules and if you break any rules, I will snatch you up without hesitating. Do you hear me?"

"Yes sir, your Honor."

"Next case."

Bj left the court house, went back to check on his drug business and then headed home for some alone time. He walked into his home with nothing on his mind but what was going to happen now that his brother is on his way home. He sat at the bar in his dining room daydreaming like always when something on his mind. He took 2 shots of Remy and picked up his phone to call his finance. He only talked to her once since he hung up the phone on her and that was only for a hot minute.

"What's up baby?"

"What do you want, Bryant?"

"Damn I can't call to talk to my soon to be wife?"

"N*gga please, I've been trying to talk to you for 2 days now and first you want to hang the phone up in my face like I'm one of them bitches you used to f*cking with, then you gots the nerve to turn your phone off for 2 days."

"Bay, I had some business to handle and I know you would be calling me trying to argue and I didn't want that. So now that my business is out of the way, I'm calling you to hear whatever it is that you want to say."

"It's not about what I have to say. It's what we have to talk about with each other."

"Everything's fine on my end. What about you?"

"Well, everything's not fine on my end cause you're there and I'm here, when we should be together. Instead of me being up all night worrying about if I'm going to be able to talk to you tomorrow or if you're going to be alive or not. Tell me right now, why is it that we have to be out here and not at home cause if you told your mother and sister-in-bro and not me then that means we right back to square one again with our trust."

"I'm not going to talk about it over the phone and you know that. You only have one more night there and then home you will be to me."

"Yeah, what ever you say."

"You miss me bay?"

"No, I don't."

"Oh, that's what it is now?"

"Yeah, that's what it is!"

"Do you stilll love me or not?"

"I'm not answering that."

"You know what, I'll talk to you when you get home then."

"No, you won't!" click and the line went dead as Bj held the phone to his ear about to say another word. He thought to himself, "This bitch is tripping and we ain't even married yet."

He went into his room, tossed his phone on the dresser and flopped down on his bed thinking about his finance as he fell asleep with his clothes and shoes stilll on.

Bj woke up to the sound of someone knocking on the door and thought he was dreaming or something until 3 more knocks came again. He wanted to ask, "Who is it?" but thought it could be the police or the feds. He walked over to the door and looked out the peep hole and didn't see anyone and as soon as he turned away from the door, the knob was turning. He looked around to see if it was something close by that he could grab in case someone other than the police was out there to protect himself casue he doesn't have any weapons in his house but there wasn't anything. He then looked out the peep hole again and caught his brother moving to the side out of the view of the peep hole. He said to himself, "This n*gga been going through for the last few months."

He stayed looking through the peep hole until he saw his brother bout to look through the peep hole from the outside and as soon as he saw him he opened the door real fast.

"N*gga what you doing?"

Nuke jumped and started laughing as he was caught off guard.

"What's up lil bro?"

"Shit, glad you're home and as I can see ain't nothing changed, huh?"

"They can hold my body, but my mind keeps thinking. You feel me?"

"I know n*gga. It runs in the blood. You feel me? Mama didn't raise no fools. That's why we stay on top."

"N*gga where that good shit at? You know I'm dying to blow back."

"N*gga is them people gone while you already trying to take more air out your lungs."

"You damn right n*gga. I ain't stopping till they flat dry."

"Your ass crazy boy. Let me wash my face then I will be down stairs, n*gga."

Bj and Nuke sat around smoking and talking for the remainder of the day. They wanted to invite the rest of the top leaders under them, but decided to keep this homecoming a secret as long as possible.

The next morning, Nuke woke up early at 7:00 am and called his attorney so he could take the paperwork to the courtroom so he could get his movement started asap.

B Real walked in the house tipsy and high with bullshit on his mind. Lately he and Monica had been arguing day in and day out for the littlest things. Today she was not feeling the vibe she and B Real been having. "It's that all you want to do is sit your fat ass around doing nothing. Damn why a n*gga can't come home to hot cooked meal or a hot bath or something?"

"Well first of all, n*ga the food was hot when you said you was on your way in 10 minutes, now here you is 2 hours later

223

walking inhere drunk and shit and talking shit."

"Bitch, who you think you are talking to like you running things around here or something?"

"You know what I'm not about to go there with you cause you're drunk and acting like you want to fight."

"But you're not going to be calling me out me name like…"

"Bitch, I'm going to do whatever the f*ck I want to do."

"No you're not, n*gga. You run them n*ggas out there, not me."

"Oh yeah?" B Real started walking up on Monica and she started backing up and asking him to please don't start. She don't feel like fighting. He reached and tried to grab her but she sidestepped out of his way. "Bay, please. Let's not go through this today. I'm already stressing and I don't want to lose our baby."

"Bitch, how do I know it's mine?"

"I can't believe you just said that you know what."

"What bitch?"

Monica started crying hard as she sat there being verbally assaulted by the n*gga who she thought she fell in love with and even choose him over her family.

"Bay, I'm sorry. Don't cry girl. Janet come here, or is it Monica?"

Monica looked up through drenched eyes as she realized what was going on. "Is this what all of this about? Huh? Is it?"

"You know what it is don't you? You f*cked him didn't you?"

"No, I didn't f*ck him. You really want to know how I know

224

him, huh? Do you really want to know?"

"Yeah, tell me. I'm all ears and if I think you're lying imam stump that bastard out of you like you're a n*gga on the streets. Now speak, bitch."

Monica stared at him for a minute not believing the words coming out of his mouth and also she's thinking about choosing her words correctly so that she won't provoke him into turning his word into action."Bay can we just talk about this in the morning when you're sober?"

"You better start talking or else," B Real said as he lifted his hand and proceeded in her direction.

"OK, look, in the beginning I was sent undercover to get close to you so that when the time was right I could set you up," she said through sniffles of tears. "but when time went by, I fell in love with you and couldn't bring myself to let them harm you. I know they gone try to kill my family now since they know that I'm on your side. Baby you have to believe me. I love you and I want to be..."

"Snake bitch. I should have blown your mother f*cking brains out," B Real said as he reached under his shirt and pulled out his 9mm and then pointed at Monica's face.

"Please let me finish..."

"Bay, my ass, all of them times I almost lost my life and you was behind it, wasn't you?"

"No, I swear I wasn't!"

"Stop lying bitch," B Real uttered as he cocked the hammer back to put a bullet in the chamber forgetting that it was one in the chamber. By him being drunk, he let the hammer slip out of his hand, which made it slam into the bullet making it go off in Monica's direction.

It was the last thing Monica heard.